MOMENT OF TRUTH

Marion didn't want to tell Rose he was not really a hero—but a Marine recruit who had been washed out of boot camp and was heading home in disgrace.

Rose didn't want to tell Marion how badly she wanted him, and how desperately scared she was of her own desire.

But they didn't have any choice. There wasn't any more time for lies, only a moment for love—before a different kind of truth, violent and raging, caught up with them. . . .

BABY BLUE MARINE

A Novel by

Max Franklin

FROM THE SCREENPLAY BY
Stanford Whitmore

A SIGNET BOOK
NEW AMERICAN LIBRARY
TIMES MIRROR

SIGNET TRADEMARK REG. U.S. PAT. OFF. AND FOREIGN COUNTRIES
REGISTERED TRADEMARK—MARCA REGISTRADA
HECHO EN CHICAGO, U.S.A.

SIGNET, SIGNET CLASSICS, MENTOR, PLUME AND MERIDIAN BOOKS
are published by The New American Library, Inc.,
1301 Avenue of the Americas, New York, New York 10019.

First Printing, March, 1976

1 2 3 4 5 6 7 8 9

PRINTED IN THE UNITED STATES OF AMERICA

Chapter 1

It was August of 1943. The stucco and tile buildings of the San Diego Marine Recruit Depot gave off shimmering heat waves, and marching feet tended to stick slightly to the asphalt-covered parade ground.

Except for his somewhat reddened face, the drill instructor seemed unaffected by the heat. His immaculately tailored Marine uniform was as crisp and knife-creased as it had been when he stepped from barracks two hours before, and even the areas around his armpits remained undarkened by perspiration. He was only about thirty, but he had the lined, weatherbeaten face of a much older man and the lithe, rock-hard body of one much younger. His left cheek bulged with a quid of Red Man, but he neither chewed nor spat. The lump of tobacco just lay there between his lower teeth and the corner of his lip.

He was drilling two platoons of Marine recruits, formed into columns of two, with an interval of three paces between platoons. The recruits' uniforms were dungarees and white sun helmets, and they were armed with M-1 rifles, carried at right-shoulder-arms. The D.I. was armed only with a swagger stick, tucked horizontally beneath his left arm. He marched to the left of the column, alongside the second platoon, his body ramrod straight, but his head turned to observe the performance of the marching men.

In a crisp voice, not particularly loud, but extremely carrying, the sergeant called, "Port—arms!"

The first platoon brought its rifles to port in perfect unison, each one canted at precisely the same angle. The rear platoon executed the maneuver with considerable individuality, the variations in timing ranging up to a couple of seconds, and the angles of the rifles in port position varying from nearly horizontal to nearly perpendicular.

The sergeant's face registered pain. "Left shoulder—arms!"

Again the first platoon performed with precision. The second not only had another time variation, but two rifles momentarily ended up on right shoulders before the men realized their errors and hurriedly shifted them to the proper side.

The D.I. momentarily closed his eyes, opened them again and bawled, "Detail—halt!"

The first platoon came to an orderly halt. The second came to a sloppy one. The sergeant did a crisp right-face.

"Right shoulder—arms!"

As soon as the command had been executed, the sergeant called, "Order—arms!"

The butt plates of the twelve rifles in the first platoon hit the asphalt at the same instant. In the second platoon there were twelve individual thumps.

"Left—think about it now—face!"

In unison the members of the first platoon pivoted to face the D.I. Ten of the second platoon swung left in ragged order, two executed right-faces, placing their backs to the D.I. Again he closed his eyes, then slowly opened them. The two blunderers sheepishly and sloppily did about-faces.

Inclining his head toward the first platoon, but with his gaze fixed on the second, the sergeant said with withering sarcasm, "Came in same day as you idiots. Wavy hair and pimples, but starting to look like Marines. But you people—thumbs up your bungs and your minds in neutral."

He approached the second platoon slowly, halted two feet from the front rank and ran his gaze over each of the twelve faces. Finally he said in a suddenly tired voice, "At ease."

The first platoon stood at ease. Six of the men in the second platoon assumed that position. Four snapped to parade rest. The other two merely sagged. Sighing, the sergeant fixed his gaze on the man immediately in front of him, one of the saggers.

"Still peeing in the sack, Mosley?"

Pop Mosley, a lanky beanpole of a man with protruding ears, owed his nickname to being the oldest recruit in the company. He was twenty-eight. Smiling nervously, he said, "You bet, sir."

Ordinarily the smile would have brought instant disciplinary action, but the D.I.'s attention was distracted by a snicker from B. J. Dobbs, the stocky recruit just to Mosley's left. Jerking his gaze that way, the sergeant roared, "Ten laps at high port!"

After a startled hesitation, Dobbs yelped, "Aye, aye, sir," and was off and running, his rifle held high before him in a two-handed grip.

The sergeant yelled after him, "Damnit, you move out when I *say* move out!"

Dobbs only increased his speed. After gazing after him disgustedly for a moment, the sergeant muttered under his breath, "Maybe keep going to Tijuana."

He moved on to Rupe Huffman, a pale, stringy eighteen-year-old. "Still saying your prayers and biting your toenails?"

"Yes, sir," the boy said, looking straight ahead.

"Old lady write yet?"

Huffman's eyes misted. "Mama's been sick, sir."

The sergeant moved on to the end of the line, halting before another eighteen-year-old. This one was neither pale nor stringy, though. He was six feet of tanned bone and muscle, with a square, handsome face. From his shaved head to his polished shoes he looked like the ideal Marine.

When the sergeant's gaze settled on him, he snapped to such rigid attention that his muscular body began to tremble.

"Marion Hedgepeth," the D.I. growled. "A recruiting poster, but land you on the beach and you'd step in dog shit."

"Yes, sir," Hedgepeth said shakily.

"One damn dog in the Pacific, and you'd find it."

He glared at the stiff, trembling shoulders in irritation. "I said *at ease*. Damn, you're just vibrating."

Without relaxing in the slightest, staring straight ahead, Hedgepeth said loudly, "I want to be a Marine, sir."

"You'll never make it, acting like a grenade's up your ass. *Relax*."

"I'm trying, sir," the big recruit said, as stiff and trembling as ever.

The drill instructor made a sour face, started to turn away, then abruptly spun back. He roared directly into the startled teen-ager's face, "Hit the deck!"

The boy slammed himself face down on the asphalt with the force of a suicide diving from a roof.

Wincing, the sergeant said, "I didn't say commit suicide."

He made an upward motion with one hand. Awkwardly and painfully Hedgepeth climbed to his feet, backed into his place in line and again froze at attention.

After examining him glumly for a time, the D.I. said, "Boy, loosen up. Get in a fight, play with yourself, do *something*." After a pause, he asked. "How many fights, so far?"

"None, sir," the boy said, staring past the sergeant's shoulder.

"Well, pick one!"

"Not pissed off at anybody, sir."

The D.I. gave his head an irritated shake. "You got the language, but that won't do it." His voice rose to a crescendo. "The idea is, Hedgepeth, *a Marine is pissed off at EVERYBODY!*"

Hedgepeth swallowed and nodded. Moving around to his left side, the D.I. leaned forward to peer into his ear. In a musing tone he said, "What I figured. Wires all tangled, couple loose."

Involuntarily the boy's left hand started to rise to his ear. With a grimace of embarrassment he lowered it again before it got there. The sergeant came back around to stand in front of him again.

"Brothers?" he inquired conversationally.

"Only child, sir."

"Thank God for small favors."

The sergeant marched back to his previous spot, four paces from the center of the second platoon's front rank, and swung to face the platoon. Before saying anything, he glanced in the direction Private Dobbs had run. Off in the distance the running man had reached the far end of the parade ground, had turned left and was haring along toward a corner.

Returning his attention to the men in front of him, the sergeant said, "Second platoon only, tench-hut!"

Ten men came to attention. Marion Hedgepeth was already at attention, and Private Dobbs was too far away to hear the command.

The sergeant said in the soft, reasoning tone of a patient farther attempting to explain something to his idiot children, "Now when I give the next command, what I want to hear is one big click. Just one. Not two. Not even one-and-a-half." He paused to let this sink in before snapping, "Port—arms! Inspection—arms!"

Eleven rifles came to port in ragged order, eleven thumbs slammed back rifle bolts to open breeches. Instead of just one click, there were four distinct ones.

The sergeant didn't even frown. He hadn't expected any better.

He said, "Okay, now you feather merchants remember about the thumb. Get it ready. Port—"

He left a long pause, as eleven thumbs were inserted into breeches to press down the clip guides while simultaneously holding back the bolts with the sides of little fingers. The bolts strained to slam shut and mangle the thumbs.

"One click now," the sergeant inserted. "Just one big one." He let suspense build, then snapped, "—arms!"

Eleven thumbs jerked from breeches, releasing the bolts to smash into the faces of the chambers. Again there were four distinct clicks.

In a sour tone the sergeant said, "Well, that's how the Army does it, but we ain't the Army, are we?"

For the first time the platoon did something in unison. As one man they roared, "No, sir!"

The D.I. looked faintly pleased. "Part of the Navy, ain't we?"

Again in perfect unison the men roared, "The best part, sir!"

The D.I. looked not only pleased, but slightly hopeful. "Hell, there may be hope yet. So we do it again. One click now. Inspection—arms!"

Bolts snapped back. When only two clicks could be heard, the sergeant looked even more hopeful.

"Port—" Again he left a long pause as thumbs were inserted into breeches before finally completing the command, "—arms!"

There was a single loud click. The D.I.'s pleased expression disappeared when he saw the agonized expression on Marion Hedgepeth's face. The big recruit's mouth opened in a soundless scream.

With mixed agony and disbelief Hedgepeth said, "My—thumb's—in—the—gun."

The sergeant stepped over to him, but offered no help, merely examining the trapped thumb critically. With his other hand Hedgepeth managed to slide back the bolt, freed his thumb and let the bolt snap closed. His face worked with pain.

"Your gun?" the D.I. inquired sarcastically. He pointed first at the rifle clutched in the big recruit's hands, then at Hedgepeth's crotch. "This is your rifle, and that is your gun. This is for shooting, and that is for fun."

"Yes, sir," Hedgepeth said miserably. "I'll remember, sir."

The sergeant returned to his former place, swung to face the troops and called, "Order—arms!"

When rifles had been returned to the men's sides, the sergeant turned his attention to the first platoon, which still stood at ease. "First platoon only," he said. "Dismissed."

As the men of the first platoon broke for barracks, the D.I. swung his attention back to the second platoon. "As a reward for your fine performance, I'm going to let you all do ten laps. When do you start, Hedgepeth?"

In a high voice Hedgepeth said, "When you say *move out,* sir."

Nodding approval, the sergeant said, "Dobbs is on his second lap." He glanced off at the racing Private Dobbs, just again reaching the far end of the parade ground, perhaps fifty yards away. "I want you all to catch him and pass him before he does five more. Understand?"

The men chorused, "Yes, sir."

"All right. *Move out!*"

The men broke and ran after Private Dobbs, their rifles held at high port.

Chapter 2

Traditionally the designation for slow-to-learn Marine recruits was "idiots." Ten of the D.I.'s idiots managed to pass Private Dobbs within the required five laps. The only failure was Rupe Huffman.

His failure, of course, brought Huffman extra punishment. Marine justice dictated that Dobbs draw extra punishment too, for allowing the other ten to pass him.

Huffman's sentence was an hour of marching in a ten-pace square in the sweltering heat, wearing a winter overcoat and cap, with his rifle at right-shoulder-arms. Dobbs's was to sing fifty choruses of "Pistol Packin' Mama" wearing an inverted bucket over his head.

Colonel Nathan Rait, the post commandant, came prowling along while the sergeant was administering this disciplinary action. The colonel was a lean, hard-bitten man who looked as though he had been plaited from rawhide. He had the face of an eagle, the movements of a cat, and he somehow gave the impression that behind his opaque sunglasses his eyes constantly blazed with fury. He had the widespread reputation among the enlisted men of being the toughest officer in the Marine Corps.

As the colonel neared, Private Huffman halted, came to attention and presented arms. The sergeant snapped to attention and saluted also. It was obvious from the rigidity of his body and the precision of his salute that despite the tradition of Marines—particularly D.I.s—fearing nothing on earth, this particular D.I. was petrified by the colonel.

The colonel snapped back a salute to both of them,

glanced at the recruit with the bucket over his head, and strode on.

The sergeant didn't relax until Colonel Rait was a safe distance beyond. Then he glanced at the perspiring Huffman, who had resumed his marching, walked over to Dobbs and smashed his swagger stick against the bucket.

"Can't hear you," he said.

Dobbs momentarily stopped singing in order to allow the concussion waves to finish vibrating through his head, then resumed again at higher volume.

Marion Hedgepeth and Pop Mosley, freshly showered and wearing skivvy shirts, came from barracks and glanced along the company street toward the parade ground. Both registered brief sympathy for the suffering Dobbs and Huffman, then Mosley shrugged and Marion turned his attention to his sore thumb. Sticking it into his mouth, he sucked on it, then pulled it out and blew on it.

Gazing down at the swollen, blue-and-yellow thumb, Pop Mosley said, "Just *got* to be a Marine, huh?"

"It's the best branch," Marion said with conviction.

"Hell it is. Know what I'd like to be? Invisible Man in the WACs. Taking showers with 'em. Nights in the barracks. Kid, I'd get more ass than a toilet seat."

Marion started to grin, then the grin was replaced by a look of alarm as he spotted the activity in front of another barracks farther along the company street. Two recruits, wearing only dog tags strung on white shoelaces above the waist, faced each other in the center of a crowd of encircling recruits. One suddenly smashed a left hook to the other's jaw.

Following Marion's gaze, Mosley also saw what was going on and headed that way. After a slight hesitation, Marion hurried to catch up with him.

By the time they reached the outer edge of the crowd, the fight was furiously underway. Despite the Marine judo lessons both men must have had by now, neither was attempting to use judo. It was simply vicious, anything-goes street fighting, as they smashed each other with fists, kicked, clawed and bit.

Appalled by the violence, Mosley and Hedgepeth looked

at each other, then in tacit accord turned and retreated toward their barracks.

Mosley said sourly, "We're all nuts. They're making us crazy. They're getting us ready."

In a querulous voice Marion asked, "Why do they want us to fight each other? We're supposed to be getting ready to fight Japs."

"That's part of it, Marion. Remember what the sergeant said? A Marine is pissed off at everybody."

"Well, I'm not going to fight my own buddies. I'll save it for the Japs."

"If you ever see any," Mosley said. "You got to make it through boot first."

That night in barracks Marion was almost incited into a fight. It began with an argument over who was going to turn out the light, and while Marion was only peripherally involved in that argument, it set the mood for the later disagreement.

The light was a bare bulb, suspended from the ceiling by a twisted double-strand wire, with a shoelace for a pull cord. That close to the ocean it got chilly at night even in August, and no one wanted to get out of his warm sack to pull the shoelace.

It started with Rupe Huffman inquiring, "Who's going to turn out the light?"

A voice from the rear end of the barracks called, "Who was the last one in?"

"Pop Mosley," Huffman said promptly. "Wasn't you, Pop?"

"Who turned it on?" Mosley countered.

"Dobbs," Huffman announced just as promptly.

Dobbs, in the bunk next to Huffman, said, "Well, I ain't getting out of this sack and freezing my ass."

Huffman said plaintively, "Dobbs, please don't use those bad words."

A recruit near the door thought of a solution that would save anyone from getting out of bed. Reaching down for one of the shoes alongside his bunk, he sat up.

"All ready on the firing line," he called. "Targets!"

He let the shoe fly. It missed the bulb, but hit the wire

it hung from just above the bulb, causing the light to swing madly.

There was instant joyful response throughout the room. A dozen shoes sailed at the bulb, all missing.

Marion, between Mosley and Huffman, left his own shoes on the floor, turned onto his back and clasped his hands behind his head to watch the bombardment.

After a time he inquired loudly, "Who's going to clean up the glass?"

Dobbs said, "That's tomorrow, Hedgepeth."

Another recruit yelled, "Banzai!" hurled a shoe and missed. But an instant later a shoe connected and the bulb burst.

Dobbs's voice crowed out in the sudden darkness, "I hit it! It was me!"

"Then you sweep up," Mosley's voice suggested.

Dobbs called, "Hey, Pop, why don't you go piss up a rope?"

In a shocked voice Rupe Huffman said, "Stop it! The language here is just terrible."

A voice from the rear end of the barracks called, "Aw, knock it off, little preacher."

Dobbs said, "Yeah, say your prayers while I yank my doodle dandy."

A muffled sob came from Huffman's bunk. In a quiet voice Marion said, "Leave him alone, Dobbs."

"Oh yeah?" Dobbs inquired belligerently.

When Marion made no answer, Dobbs didn't push it and the matter died. There was a long silence, eventually broken by low-toned singing from near the door, an off-key rendition of "Paper Doll."

The singer gradually increased his volume. As he reached the line, "Then those flirty-flirty guys, with their flirty-flirty eyes——" Pop Mosley loudly interrupted with, "That the only song you know?"

The singing stopped. After a moment of silence the singer inquired belligerently, "Wanta make something of it?"

Mosley said, "Too cold to turn off the light, too cold to fight."

The logic of that seemed to be convincing, because after a short pause, the singer said in an entirely cheerful voice, "Hey, you really think they're putting something in our coffee?"

From the rear of the room someone called, "Well, it sure as hell ain't Spanish fly."

There were a number of snickers, then silence. After a time Marion rolled over to face Pop Mosley's way and asked in a low voice, "What's going to happen, Pop?"

"I'm going to fart twice and go to sleep."

"I'm serious, Pop."

Mosley emitted a sigh. After considerable silence, he said, "I'm surprised they let us get this far."

In an intense tone Marion said, "Everybody's in the war. All that's back home are old men and little kids."

"And pussy. Tons of it."

There was an indignant gasp from the bunk on the other side of Marion, containing Rupe Huffman.

The recruit who had been singing called, "Hey, knock it off, huh?"

Ignoring him, Marion said, "Thing is, my dad was a Marine. Uniform still fits him, too. But I guess you wouldn't mind the Army, would you, Pop?"

"Hell, the Army takes me and I still don't know left from right, and flood the old sack every night."

After a period of shocked silence, Marion said, "You've been doing it *on purpose?*"

There was the sound of Mosley fumbling beneath his pillow, then Marion could dimly see him groping into one of his shoes alongside the bunk. Apparently it was a cigarette lighter he took from the shoe, because a moment later it flared. He leaned toward the younger man and held the flame in front of the photograph he had taken from beneath his pillow, canting the picture toward Marion. It was of a smiling, lusciously built blonde in a bathing suit.

"That's what's back home, kid," Mosley said.

Staring at the photograph in admiration, Marion said in an awed voice, "This is your wife?"

Nodding, Mosley said, "Don't ask me how I got so lucky."

He canted the picture toward himself and gazed at it in the flickering light. In a wry tone he said, "Trouble is, she gets lonesome easy."

He let the lighter go out, dropped it back into his shoe and Marion could hear his pillow rustle as he shoved the photograph back under it. There was a long period of silence, then Mosley said with sudden desperation, "I got to get home *fast.*"

From near the door the recruit who had been singing yelled, "Hey, I'm trying to sleep!"

Mosley said, "War's a crock anyway. You'll see."

Marion, who had raised on one elbow to see the photograph, settled back onto his side. In a near whisper he said, "Half the town turned out to see me off. 'Course that's not many people, but still—" He let it trail off, then suddenly changed direction to ask, "What kind of discharge, Pop?"

"Baby Blue Marine. Official idiot."

"I ain't no idiot," Marion said without much conviction.

The ex-singer yelled, "Will you guys shut the Christ up!"

For the first time since arriving at camp, Marion lost his temper. Flinging back his covers, he bounced to his feet.

"You want to go a couple of rounds?" he flared into the darkness.

There was silence from the direction the yell had come. Mosley said indulgently, "Knock it off, kid."

Still poised, his fists knotted, Marion continued to glare into the darkness in the general direction from which the ex-singer's voice had come. When there continued to be no response, he climbed back into bed.

Mosley said, "All I know is I'm living in the idiot barracks with the idiots, and it's all right with me."

Marion shifted onto his back and lay staring at the ceiling. The room became silent except for a cough from near the rear wall, the creak of bedsprings as someone turned over, and a soft snore. Then, from the bunk on his opposite side from Pop Mosley's, Marion heard a sniffle and a soft, nearly inaudible moan of, "Mama, oh, Mama."

Marion whispered, "It's going to be all right, Rupe. Things work out."

Chapter 3

The following morning the recruits were ordered to fall in with full field packs and rifles. After inspection they were loaded aboard two-and-a-half-ton trucks and were driven north to La Jolla, where the Marine rifle range was located. There they were quartered in pyramidal tents, and after lunch were marched to the range.

There were three degrees of qualification with the M-1 rifle—marksman, sharpshooter and expert—and it was necessary to score at least marksman before you could graduate from boot camp. Today was the first time this particular bunch of recruits had attempted to qualify. It was not expected that everyone would make it on the first attempt, but those who didn't could look forward to considerable hazing from their D.I.s after each failure.

Marion Hedgepeth and Pop Mosley got positions on the firing line next to each other, which gave them the same coach, a bull-necked sergeant in his mid-thirties. He handed them ammunition clips, watched them load, and instructed them to put rounds in their chambers.

The first firing position was offhand, which meant standing. The coach explained that they would fire at the nearest targets first, then progressively work up to maximum range. The targets at one-hundred-yard range were already up from the butts.

A crisp voice from their right called, "Ready on the right." A voice from the opposite direction called, "Ready on the left." Marion's and Mosley's coach called, "Ready on the firing line."

The range officer ordered, "Aim!"

Marion raised his rifle to his shoulder and tried, as he

had been instructed, to balance the bull's-eye on the front sight like a ball on the nose of a performing seal. It was difficult to hold the nine-pound weapon steady, though, and the sight kept veering both back and forth and up and down.

"Commence firing," the range officer commanded.

Marion settled the rifle butt more firmly against his shoulder and peered through the sight. It continued to veer widely. Finally he squeezed the trigger just as the sight moved from left to right across the bull's-eye, then squeezed it again when it swung back.

He involuntarily squeezed it a third time without even aiming when the coach yelled in his ear, "This is supposed to be rapid fire, Hedgepeth!"

He squeezed off two more quick shots in the general direction of the target.

To his right Pop Mosley got five shots off before Marion fired his first one. But his speed was because he didn't bother to aim. He fired with his eyes closed.

The targets sank down into the butts and spotting flags began to wave. Marion had scored one hit in the outer ring of the target. Mosley had scored zero.

Neither man did much better either kneeling, seated or in prone position, although Mosley unexpectedly got a bull's-eye at five hundred yards seated. It was his only shot that even hit the target.

Just before prone firing began, the coach knelt next to Marion and asked, "Son, you ever fired before?"

"B-B gun, sir."

"Hit anything?" the sergeant inquired.

"Oh, yes, sir. I broke a lot of bottles."

"Maybe you'd better pretend you're shooting at bottles," the coach suggested.

The advice didn't do much good. Marion got two hits in the outer rings at one hundred yards, and never more than one hit each at farther ranges.

In the trucks on the way back to boot camp that evening the men unbuckled their harnesses and slipped off their field packs. When they arrived back at camp, they simply carried the packs in their hands by the harnesses instead of buckling them back on as they climbed from the trucks. This was per instructions, so that the rifle scores chalked on their backs could be seen.

Marion Hedgepeth, Pop Mosley, B. J. Dobbs and Rupe Huffman all had huge Xs chalked across their backs, indicating they had failed to qualify.

As Marion and Mosley trudged side by side toward barracks, Mosley was as cheerful as ever, but Marion was sunk in gloom. Both ran their gazes over some of the scores on the backs of men walking in front of them.

"Look at that," Mosley said with no evidence of envy in his voice. "Two twenty-four. Make him a sniper, and good luck."

"There's a one ninety-one," Marion said in a doleful voice. "He made it."

The acute misery in his voice made Mosley glance at him. "Don't take it so hard, kid," he advised. "It's not the end of the world."

"Close," Marion said. "You can't be a Marine without qualifying."

"Yeah," Mosley said in a tone of satisfaction.

Marion looked at him, momentarily distracted from his own misery by the realization of what the other's tone implied. "You didn't try," he accused.

"I tried as hard as a man can—not to qualify," Mosley told him cheerfully.

Marion shook his head, not so much in disapproval as in wonderment that anyone could not want to be a Marine.

They reached the barracks and halted outside to check the scores of the men who had been walking behind them as they went by. As qualifying score after qualifying score passed by, Marion's expression became progressively more miserable.

"Hey, cheer up," Mosley said. "You'll make it next time."

The younger man shook his head. "I just can't shoot."

Examining him critically, Mosley said, "You sure look like a Marine, kid. Ever play football?"

"Yeah, in high school."

"Any good?"

"All conference end."

"No fooling?" Unhooking his canteen from his web belt, Mosley faded back, holding the canteen in its canvas cover like a football. "Score tied, ten seconds to go. We need a touchdown."

Marion showed mild interest, then made a face and shook his head.

"Come on, buddy," Mosley urged, bringing the canteen back over his shoulder in pass position. "Nine seconds—eight—and the crowd's screaming!"

Caught up in the make-believe, momentarily forgetting his troubles, Marion allowed a grin to form on his face. Then he was racing along the company street toward an imaginary goal line, looking back over his shoulder as he ran.

"Four seconds now!" Mosley shouted. "And there it goes!"

He heaved the canteen, watched it arch high in the air and begin to come down, then emitted a gasp of alarm as his gaze settled on the figure striding along just beyond both the descending canteen and Private Hedgepeth.

Marion, running at full speed, his head turned backward, made a spectacular over-the-shoulder catch. An instant later there was a bone-crunching collision with someone in khaki. Marion and the man he collided with both went down, but the big recruit held onto the canteen-football.

Holding up the canteen, he triumphantly announced, "Touchdown!"

Then, still seated spraddle-legged, he looked over his shoulder to see who he had run into.

Colonel Nathan Rait, one lens of his sunglasses shattered to expose a furiously blazing eye, lay sprawled on his elbows. The eye fixed on Marion like that of a mongoose studying a cobra.

Hurriedly jumping to his feet, Marion ran over to offer the camp commandant a helping hand up. It was rejected with such blistering invective that the recruit backed away and snapped to terrified attention, the canteen still held in his left hand. As the colonel slowly climbed to his feet, Marion's drill instructor appeared on the scene.

The colonel roared, "Have that man's service record on my desk tomorrow morning, Sergeant!"

Snapping to rigid attention, the D.I. said, "Yes, sir," and saluted.

The colonel returned the salute, let his exposed eye glitter at Marion once more, then strode off.

Relaxing, the sergeant fixed Marion with two glittering eyes, "Tell me about it, Hedgepeth," he said softly. "I didn't see what happened, but I'm curious. How did you manage to knock a full bird colonel on his ass?"

On graduation day there was a lot of activity around the depot's main gate area. Parents, girl friends and wives were there in droves to congratulate the graduates. There was also a group of non-graduates waiting to board a base bus to take them to the San Diego bus depot.

One pair of proud parents, middle-aged and well dressed, were alternately taking pictures of each other with their son, who wore brand-new PFC stripes and a sharpshooter's medal. As the mother surrendered the Brownie camera to her husband and placed herself alongside the new Marine, her gaze fell on the waiting group of nongraduates.

The men's appearance was startling. Carrying only small bags as luggage—too small to contain any additional clothing other than a change of socks and underwear—they wore electric baby-blue cotton suits and matching caps. Humiliated for all the world to see, with their shaved heads and ridiculous uniforms they looked like comic opera characters playing the roles of jailbirds.

The woman said, "Junior, who are those people?"

Glancing that way, the PFC said, "The Baby Blues? Just the shitheads going home."

The open-mouthed shock with which both his parents received this made the new Marine realize too late what eight weeks of barracks room talk had done to his vocabulary. Embarrassedly he tried to amend it by saying hurriedly, "I mean the guys who flunked out. The rejects."

The bus pulled up and its door opened. The rejects started to board.

In a smoldering voice Marion Hedgepeth said, "That colonel's got some sense of humor."

Rupe Huffman said, "I just bet the general don't know. Made us send our *good* clothes home. Wait'll Mama sees. She'll write President Roosevelt."

Pop Mosley said smugly, "Mine fits fine." He jerked his head in the direction of the mixture of parents, girls and newly uniformed Marines. "Quit bitching and take a look."

The other two looked that way. "What about it?" Marion asked.

"So they got their uniforms. Aren't the mothers proud? Six months to a year their windows will be full of gold stars, and their loving sons full of worms."

"All aboard," the bus driver called.

They turned to find they were the only three not yet loaded. As they climbed aboard, the reject Marion had once challenged to a fight began to sing "Paper Doll."

"Jesus," Pop Mosley said. "He still only knows one tune. But we only have to listen as far as San Diego."

Overhearing, the man stopped singing and said belligerently, "Want to make something out of it, Mosley?"

"Aw, knock it off," Mosley said in a bored voice. "You don't have to prove how tough you are anymore by fighting everybody in sight. Fact, you don't have to fight *anybody*."

The other man looked thoughtful, then shrugged. The three continued on to the rear, where the only remaining seats were, and seated themselves together on the long back seat.

The singer resumed: "When I come home at night, she will be waiting—She'll be the truest doll in all the world—I'd rather have a paper doll to call my own, than a good-for-nothing real-life doll."

Chapter 4

Rupe Huffman, Pop Mosley and B. J. Dobbs were scheduled to take the same eastbound bus from San Diego, as Huffman lived in Tucson, Arizona, Mosley near El Paso, and Dobbs just outside of New Orleans. Marion Hedgepeth, whose home was Crystal City, Missouri, had to take a northbound bus to Los Angeles, where he would change to one that followed Route 66 to St. Louis, then change again to a local which would take him the last forty miles south of St. Louis to home. Marion therefore had to say good-bye to his buddies at the San Diego bus depot.

His bus was scheduled out first, from the depot's lower level. The three others went downstairs with him to see him aboard. There was a fifteen-minute wait, and they stood on the loading ramp in awkward silence.

Finally, catching his reflection in the mirrored front of a gum machine, Marion made a face and said, "Hate going home looking this way."

"Rather a pine box with a flag?" Mosley asked.

Rupe Huffman said, "Hey, we got each other's addresses?"

Marion said, "I got you guys."

"Tear 'em up," Mosley advised cynically. "We'll never see each other again."

With a touch of sadness Marion realized this was true. He knew he would never write any of them, or even look them up if he happened to pass through their towns, because they had nothing to share but shame. Then his sadness changed to apprehension as he spotted a pair of Navy shore patrolmen approaching along the loading ramp.

"Hey," he said to the others, jerking his head in that direction.

The other three looked, and their expressions instantly registered a mixture of fear and antagonism. The two shore patrolmen strolled closer, clubs dangling from their wrists, eyeing the group of rejects with open contempt. Both were in their early twenties, identically large and squarely built, but totally different in coloring. One was redheaded and freckled, the other dark and swarthy.

Halting a few feet away, they deliberately looked the four rejects up and down. The redhead said, "Boy, the things you see when you ain't got a gun."

The swarthy man said, "Hey, you psychos and mama's boys like to line up and kiss my ass?"

"Mark off a spot," Mosley said agreeably. "You're all ass."

The S.P.'s dark face turned even darker. Gripping his club, he started to raise it, but his partner put a restraining hand on his wrist. Grinning at Mosely sardonically, the redhead said, "Well, listen to the old salt."

Grinning just as sardonically, Mosley said, "In a couple of days the old salt's going to be screwing his wife while you two deck apes hang around heads slugging fruits."

The swarthy man said, "Better'n getting a dose like your old lady'll give you."

This time it was Mosely's face that darkened. He started toward the shore patrolman, but Marion stuck out a thick arm to block his way.

"Come on, Pop," he said soothingly. "They just got nothing better to do."

Mosley looked down at the arm blocking his way, pressed his chest against it, but it was like trying to push aside an oak limb. Shrugging, he subsided.

The two shore patrolmen turned their attention to the big reject. The contrast between his Marine-like build and the ridiculous outfit he wore seemed to strike them as funny, because both grinned. Then the redhead chuckled, his partner chuckled also, and suddenly both were roaring with laughter.

Humiliated and angry, Marion could think of nothing

to do except stand there redfaced and endure the laughter. Eventually it eased off to a mere snickering, and the two men moved on, their snickers still audible until they disappeared from sight up the stairs to the upper level.

At that moment the bus to Los Angeles pulled up, halting next to the loading ramp a dozen yards beyond where the four were standing. Immediately passengers waiting to board crowded around the door.

Marion said awkwardly, "Well, I better get in line if I want to make my bus."

Rupe Huffman held out his hand. "Good luck, Hedgepeth."

Gripping the hand, Marion said, "Bye, Rupe. Hello to your mom."

"Take it easy now," B. J. Dobbs said, thrusting out his hand. "See you at the PX."

"Yeah," Marion said.

Huffman said, "Semper Fi, buddy."

"We got a scholar," Dobbs said, clapping the pale boy on the back. "He ain't a preacher after all. He's a priest."

Everyone smiled obediently, in the vain hope of lessening the pain of parting. Marion held out his hand to Pop Mosley. "So long, Pop."

Gripping the proffered hand firmly, Mosley said, "When it's all over, nobody's going to give a damn if you were a hero or a Four-F. So just stay alive. It's all a crock anyway."

Marion smiled wanly, mentally disagreeing, but not wanting to part on a note of disagreement. He merely said, "Best to your pretty wife."

Turning, he shifted his small bag from his left to his right hand and went over to stand at the end of the line of passengers boarding the bus.

He found a seat on the aisle near the rear, next to a black sailor. The sailor looked at his baby blue uniform, leaned his head against the back of his seat and closed his eyes.

Properly rebuffed, Marion glanced around at the other passengers. Most were in civilian clothes, but there were eight other uniforms. In the seat immediately in front of him two Army corporals, both loudly drunk, were passing a pint of whiskey back and forth. Four Army privates and a buck sergeant were seated in the long back seat. A staff sergeant in the aisle seat immediately in front of them, on the opposite side of the aisle from Marion, seemed to be with them, because he was seated sidewise, feet in the aisle, talking to them. That put his back to his seatmate, a thin, very plain woman in her mid-twenties who could have played the stage part of a frustrated spinster without requiring acting lessons.

As the bus started to move, Hedgepeth peered past the black sailor through the window. Huffman, Dobbs and Mosley were standing outside, looking up at the window. They all smiled and waved. He waved back.

One of the corporals in front of him said to his buddy in a whiskey-slurred voice, "Hey, you remember the lungs on that blonde? Or was it a redhead?" After a moment of thought, he continued, "Hell with it. Full of rats and Spam. Christ, if that old minister could see me now, drunker'n a skunk."

That seemed to be a mixture of recollections, Marion thought, wondering if the man's seatmate had the vaguest idea of what he was talking about. Apparently he did, because he said, "Redhead. Old boy probably wouldn't be surprised. Figured you were going to hell anyway."

By the time they reached the open highway, a party had started at the rear of the bus. One of the servicemen broke out a bottle of Southern Comfort and passed it around. Marion heard the staff sergeant offer a drink to the thin woman seated next to him, and heard her surprised, "Oh, I don't think I ought."

"Why not?" the sergeant inquired. "Pretend you're the USO. You're supposed to cheer up the troops."

She emitted a nervous giggle. "Well, maybe a little one," she said timidly.

An hour later the party was in full swing. The spinsterish woman, fortified by several drinks, was having the time of her life as the center of attraction amid six servicemen, probably the first male attention she had ever received.

Marion heard the staff sergeant say, "You're okay, Betty Grable. Hey, pass the Southern Comfort. Who'n hell said war's hell anyway?"

Wishing he could join in the revelry, but knowing there was no chance of his being invited, Marion closed his ears to it and attempted to distract himself by taking out his wallet and looking at photographs.

One was of his parents, taken the day before he left home. They stood side by side in the front yard of the house where he had been born and had grown up, smiling into the camera. His father was an older version of himself, with the same Marine-like build and a square, rather good-looking face. His mother was a still pretty woman with a well-rounded figure just beginning to grow plump.

They wouldn't be smiling like that when he got home, he thought glumly. When the photograph was taken, they hadn't know they had an idiot son.

It was just turning dark when they reached the Los Angeles bus depot. Disembarking, Marion carried his little canvas bag into the waiting room and looked around until he spotted a sign reading INFORMATION above a circular counter. A trim, gray-haired woman stood behind the counter and a line of servicemen stood before it. The line was moving fast, and only two men were ahead of him by the time Marion had walked across the room.

The first man in line, a sailor, asked, "Kansas City?"

"Gate two, three hours," the woman said crisply.

As the sailor moved off, the Marine behind him asked, "Nashville?"

"Gate two, three hours."

As the Marine moved away, the woman regarded Marion's wretched suit and cap with surprise. She obviously didn't recognize its significance, because the question she asked him suggested that she was hazarding the guess that he was a sailor ashore from some foreign ship.

"You speak English?"

Puzzled, he nodded. "St. Louis?"

"Gate two, three hours."

Muttering thanks, he moved away, looked around again

until he spotted gate two, then decided to put his bag in a coin locker. After disposing of it, he decided he was hungry and went into the depot coffee chop. He took a seat at the counter.

A radio behind the counter was blaring a song that made Marion wince. It was a thing called "I'll Be Back in a Year, Little Darling," the lyric of which purportedly was being sung by a freshly drafted young man, telling his girl friend good-by just before departing for camp. It had become popular during the early days of the draft, before the country was at war, and inductees could look forward to being released from service after only one year of military duty. Unaccountably, now that all servicemen were in for the duration unless discharged for special circumstances, the piece was still polluting the airwaves.

A young waitress appeared on the other side of the counter, examined Marion's uniform curiously and said, "What'll it be?"

He ordered a hamburger and a glass of milk.

It was 8:00 P.M when he walked out of the bus station. His bus wasn't scheduled to leave until 10:30. Outside he paused to look around.

As in all big cities where servicemen were constantly streaming through town, the bus station had become the focal point for the parasitical businesses that preyed on servicemen. Within Marion's view there were a half-dozen B-girl bars, a taxi-dance hall, a tattoo parlor and a pinball arcade.

A good many people were lounging in front of the depot. Some probably were merely killing time while waiting for buses, but several young women in spike heels, low-cut blouses and too-heavy makeup were identifiable as prostitutes by the inviting way they eyed passing servicemen. There was also a pair of girls who couldn't have been more than sixteen, dressed in skirts, sweaters and bobby sox, eyeing passing servicemen with equal invitation. They were V-girls, he realized with fascination. He had heard of them, because they were a common subject of barracks conversation—young girls whose contribution to the war effort was to offer their bodies to any serviceman who happened along, simply to lift his morale—but these were the first he had ever seen.

As he watched, two sailors stopped to speak to them, and they walked off holding the sailors' arms.

Two young Mexicans walked by wearing loudly checked suits with thigh-length jackets with widely padded shoulders and peg-top trousers tapering to narrow cuffs. They were the first zoot-suiters Marion had ever seen, and he gazed at them as though seeing beings from another planet. They had never seen anything like his outfit either. They gazed back as though *he* were from another planet.

An Army lieutenant with terrible burn scars on his face passed by. Marion snapped to attention and saluted. The man gave him a surprised look and failed to return the salute.

Marion walked along the street until he was out of the bus terminal area, found a quiet-looking bar and went in.

Chapter 5

Four Army privates were seated together in a booth. The only other two customers were seated at the bar. Near the right end there was a pretty young woman with curling brown hair, wearing a conservative suit, who looked as though she might be an office secretary. In the bar's center was an Army second lieutenant. Marion took a stool at the far left end.

The bartender, a glum-looking man of middle-age, regarded the baby blue outfit with the puzzlement Marion was becoming used to.

"Beer, please," Marion said.

He was afraid the man was going to ask for his I.D., because the drinking age in California was twenty-one, but he only said, "Twenty-five."

"Yes, sir," Marion said, producing a quarter and laying it on the bar.

The bartender rang it up before delivering an opened bottle of beer. No glass came with the bottle, and Marion was too timid to ask for one.

He said, "Thank you."

The bartender moved away without answering. Marion took a sip of beer and made a face. He didn't particularly like beer, but it would have embarrassed him to ask for a soft drink.

As he set down the bottle, he caught his reflection in the back-bar mirror and hurriedly averted his gaze. To avoid looking at himself, he glanced at the other two customers. The lieutenant was also drinking beer, but he had a glass. The girl was sipping something pink and frothy in a stemmed glass.

As he watched, the lieutenant emptied the rest of his bottle into the glass, picked up the glass and walked along the bar to seat himself next to the girl. She paid no attention to him. After a moment he turned his head to say something to her. She looked straight ahead, giving no indication that she had even heard him. He said something else; when she continued totally ignoring him, he reddened, drained his glass and walked out.

Interested in the vignette, he followed the lieutenant's retreating form with his gaze. A Marine corporal entered as the lieutenant exited, the two exchanging salutes as they passed.

Marion turned back to face his reflection and took another sip of beer.

As he set down the bottle, he became peripherally aware of the corporal taking the stool to his right. Shifting his gaze that way, the first thing he saw was the Marine Raider's death's-head patch sewn above the corporal stripes.

Awed to be in the presence of one of the famed Raiders, he surreptitiously examined the man. The corporal was about the same build as Marion but with a longer and narrower face and close-cropped snow-white hair that was rather startling above his youthful face. His gray eyes struck Marion as icy, yet fire seemed to smolder deeply within them.

Marion sneaked a look at the man's ribbons, noting that he had disdained to wear the common American Theater ribbon that virtually every serviceman had. He wore the Presidential Unit Citation with star, the Asiatic Theater Ribbon with two stars, the Purple Heart, and above those, the Navy Cross.

"Hello, sir," Marion ventured in a hero-worshipping voice.

The Raider glanced at and through him, then said to the approaching bartender in a strangely soft voice, "Beer."

Fumbling in his pocket, Marion brought out another quarter and laid it on the bar. "I'd like to treat."

Again looking through him, the corporal gave a faint, indifferent nod. The barkeep rang up the quarter and delivered a bottle of beer, again without a glass. Instead of drinking, the corporal merely gripped the bottle with his left hand and began scraping a strip from the label with his right forefinger. He concentrated on the work, as though it were a necessary job.

"You're a Raider, I see, sir," Marion said deferentially.

There was no response.

"I learned the patches," Marion offered.

There was still no response.

"I've been in boot camp," Marion continued. "Didn't have what it takes, whatever it is. So home, and I guess the Army."

The Raider glanced at him finally, then returned his attention to the job of scraping off the label. "You just came from Dago?" he inquired in the same soft voice in which he had ordered the beer.

"Yes, sir," Marion said, pleased at finally getting some response. "They made us wear this. Shame us."

Suddenly remembering he was wearing a cap in the presence of a hero, Marion snatched it off. The Raider looked at him again, this time not through him, but actually noticing him. He said, "Look like a Marine to me."

Marion felt as grateful as a patted puppy. The Raider returned his attention to scraping the label.

Marion said tentatively, "Sir, you mind if—? Sir, what's it like out there in the South Pacific?"

Concentrating on his work, the Raider said indifferently, "Weather's nice. Warm, a little rain every day. Sunsets. Gets dark just like that."

"But big mosquitos, huh?"

"Peckers as big as your thumb."

Marion debated asking a more personal question, afraid he might offend the man, but finally couldn't resist asking, "Probably killed some Japs."

"Everybody did," the Raider said, again indifferently.

Encouraged, Marion asked another personal question. "Hope you don't mind my asking, but where'd you get wounded?"

A crooked smile briefly showed on the man's face. "Where it doesn't show."

"No, I—I meant the island."

"They're all the same."

Conversation lapsed. Marion took another sip of beer while trying to think of some way to resume it. Finally something else occurred to him. "Guess you got thirty days now, huh?"

"Had," the corporal said.

"Oh. Bet they have you teach bayonet now, or——"

Impaling him with suddenly blazing eyes, the Raider interrupted. "They're sending me back."

Appalled, Marion stared at him. In a high voice he said, "That don't seem fair." He pointed to the man's ribbons. "Purple Heart and the Navy Cross, and only thing's higher than that's the Congressional Medal of Honor."

The fire in the man's eyes died and he looked faintly amused. "Learned those too, huh?"

"Yes, sir. You know it don't seem right. They're sending you back and I get to go home."

A slight flaring of the corporal's nostrils suggested that he agreed that it wasn't right. But all he said, apropos of nothing, was, "In a month I'm going to be twenty-one."

Conversation lapsed again. Suddenly the Raider glanced around and spotted the girl at the far end of the bar. He examined her with growing interest.

His gaze still on the girl, he asked, "You like Scotch, kid?"

"Scotch whiskey?"

"It's whiskey."

Marion said embarrassedly, "Only tried whiskey once. Sicker'n a dog."

The Raider wrenched his gaze from the girl and turned his head to face Marion. Smiling twistedly, he said, "I like you, kid. Stop calling me sir. My name is Andy."

"Yes, sir. I mean Andy. I'm Marion."

Pushing the untouched bottle of beer in front of Marion, Andy said, "Drink it or leave it, Marion. I'm after top shelf."

"How's that, sir? I mean Andy."

"Now this is in two parts, so pay attention." He patted

his right-hand jacket pocket. "My Scotch pocket. Dime, two nickels, and *six* pennies. Second part's the bulkhead stare and what I'm thinking about. Know what I'm thinking about?"

"What?"

"My dead buddies."

Marion didn't have the slightest idea what he was talking about, and he had no opportunity to inquire because the Raider abruptly got up and strode toward the girl at the opposite end of the bar.

Marion could see the young woman's back stiffen in anticipation of another pickup attempt. But Andy went right past her to seat himself on the stool to her right. A few moments later, from what shortly developed, Marion realized he had deliberately placed himself on that side instead of to her left so that she couldn't fail to see the death's-head shoulder patch and the combat decorations, if she ever deigned to look at him.

Andy did not so much as glance at the girl. Since she had seen him come from the opposite end of the bar, she must have been puzzled as to why he made the move if he wasn't trying to pick her up, but after a few moments of his continuing to ignore her totally, she seemed to decide she wasn't his target, because she visibly relaxed. Perhaps she concluded that he was merely eccentric, or a little drunk. She took a sip of her pink cocktail.

When the bartender came over, Andy asked, "How much is Scotch?"

"Fifty."

"Beer?"

He had just ordered a beer at the other end of the counter, but apparently the bartender figured it was no business of his if the Marine wanted to play games. He said patiently, "Quarter."

"I'll have a beer."

He emptied his pocket of the dime, two nickels and six pennies. Pushing twenty-five cents to the bartender, he picked up the extra penny, contemplated it with wry amusement, then dropped it back in his pocket.

The young woman looked straight ahead as the bartender rang up the money and delivered a bottle of beer. But as Andy raised it to his lips, her eyes flicked sidewise long enough to glimpse his shoulder patch and ribbons.

The glance hooked her. She did her best to resist a second glance at the Marine hero who had just enough money for one beer, but inevitably her gaze drifted sidewise again. He was cuddling the bottle in a two-handed grip suggesting he planned to nurse it for a long time, perhaps through the evening, and was gazing vacantly at nothing with a "bulkhead stare."

Marion, watching in fascination, could almost read the girl's thoughts. She probably had decided the Marine's erratic behavior was due to combat fatigue. And she looked as though she was consumed by guilt at drinking an expensive cocktail while the shattered hero next to her had to nurse a single beer.

She gave in. Turning her head, she said something to Andy that Marion couldn't hear. The corporal blinked, slowly emerged from his trance, and looked at her as though just now becoming aware that someone was seated next to him. He said, "What?"

She repeated herself, again in too low a voice for Marion to make out what she said. But he clearly heard Andy's reply. "My dead buddies."

He resumed his bulkhead stare. She gazed at him, now totally hooked. Again she said something, and this time she lifted the beer bottle from his grip and set it, with an air of finality, in the little trough at the rear of the bar.

Andy gradually came out of his trance again. His eyes cleared and for the first time he really looked at her, the look suggesting that he just now was realizing it was a girl sitting next to him, and a quite attractive girl at that.

"All right," he said.

She signaled to the bartender and said, this time loudly enough for Marion to hear, "Give the corporal whatever he wants."

Andy's left hand lightly gripped the girl's wrist, and

his right forefinger pointed at Marion at the opposite end of the bar. "My buddy," he said.

She looked somewhat disconcerted, but she couldn't very well refuse to include the hero's buddy. She nodded.

Releasing the girl's wrist, Andy motioned Marion to join them. The invitation astonished him, but he was not about to question his good luck. Leaving both his own half-empty beer bottle and Andy's untouched one, he went to the other end of the bar.

Chapter 6

The girl introduced herself as Betty. She didn't offer a last name, and neither did the two men. After one drink at the bar, she suggested moving to a booth. Marion sat alone on one side of the booth, Andy and Betty on the other.

The rest of the evening became progressively hazier to Marion. Drinks kept coming at a dizzying rate, and he kept gulping them down. Andy and Betty were drinking just as many, but it didn't seem to affect either of them the way it was hitting him.

Even through his drunkenness Marion became aware by the way Betty was looking at Andy that he was scoring heavily with her, but Andy's reaction puzzled him. While polite to her, he seemed indifferent to the obvious vibes she was throwing out. He paid much more attention to Marion, drawing him out about his home town, his family, and his future plans.

Perversely her inability to rouse Andy's interest seemed to fascinate the girl. She must have regarded it as a challenge, because by the time they had consumed several drinks, she was literally throwing herself at him.

Marion had entirely forgotten about the time when, through his alcoholic haze, he heard Andy ask, "Doesn't your bus leave at ten-thirty, Marion?"

Marion gazed at his new buddy, seeing his face fluctuate at the end of a long tunnel. "Bus?" he inquired thickly.

"He's smashed," Andy said to Betty. "I'd better get him to the bus station. It's almost ten."

"We'll both take him," she said. "After we see him off, we can go to my place for coffee or something."

Rising from the booth, he smiled down at her. "Thanks, but I'm taking off shortly too."

In a disappointed voice she said, "Well, at least I can walk to the bus depot with you."

She started to slide across the booth, but he dropped an arresting hand on her shoulder. "My buddy and I have some private business. Thanks for the drinks."

She stared up at him without understanding, her face slightly flushed. "You mean this is good-bye?"

"Uh-huh. Take care."

He helped Marion from the booth. The younger man had difficulty standing. Andy drew Marion's left arm across his shoulders and guided him toward the door. The girl gazed after them, but Andy never glanced back.

Outside Andy got a firm grip around Marion's waist and steered the staggering youth in the direction of the bus depot.

"Andy, I don't get it," Marion said drunkenly. "I mean you were doing great, and why'd you want me?"

The bus depot was straight ahead along the main street they were on, but at the corner Andy steered Marion left down a narrow side street.

Marion said, "You know she liked you. I could tell."

They stopped at the mouth of an alley. Andy said, "Don't feel so good, do you, buddy?"

After thinking about it, Marion said, "Now that you mention." He emitted a slight groan. "Oh, Andy, I'm dizzy and sick."

"Not used to Scotch," Andy said sympathetically.

"Never again," Marion assured him, weaving slightly despite being supported against his buddy. He began to wonder why they didn't move on instead of just standing there.

"Scotch is nothing," Andy said. "Knew a guy drank shoe polish."

Marion felt his stomach constrict.

"Melt it, strain it through bread."

Marion's stomach lurched.

"Kiwi. Cordovan."

In a sick voice Marion said, "Shoe polish!"

The nearest street lamp was across the street a quarter block away, but it threw enough glow for Andy to make out that the drunken youth's face had completely drained of color.

"Come on, get rid of it," he said, and guided Marion into the alley.

Buildings blocked the light from the distant street lamp from entering the alley. It was pitch dark in there.

As he stumbled deeper into the darkness, Marion moaned, "Oh, Andy, I just want to die."

"Come on," Andy said, leading him over to a trash can and bending him over it.

Marion emptied his stomach into the can. He was beginning to feel a little better when he straightened up. But then the hard edge of a palm smashed into the side of his neck from behind, and he abruptly passed out.

Marion awakened lying flat on his back. It was a slow awakening. For a time he lay with his eyes closed, conscious only of an aching head and an aching neck, but not even aware of where he was. Then he opened his eyes, gazed puzzledly up at stars, and dimly began to remember.

Andy had hit him from behind with a judo chop, he realized with shock and disappointment. The thought jerked him to a seated position, the sudden movement nearly bursting his head. He waited, eyes pressed tightly shut, until the pain subsided to a dull ache, then reopened his eyes and started to raise his right hand to gingerly feel his neck.

It never got there, because he felt something clenched in the hand and brought it in front of his eyes to examine it. It was money—a single bill. In the darkness it was hard to make out the denomination, but he finally detected that it was a two-dollar bill.

Bewildered, he reached to tuck it into his jacket pocket and got a second shock. He had been stripped to his underwear and shoes.

Struggling to his feet, he looked around. With relief he spotted a neatly folded pile of clothing next to a nearby trash can. But when he bent over it, he discovered it was not his baby blue outfit. It was the Raider's uniform, complete with tie, cap and ribbons.

"Oh, my God!" he said, staring around wildly. "Andy? Andyyy!"

There was no answer. Then it hit him. Even before he patted the uniform pockets and found them empty, he knew Andy had taken not only his clothing but his papers and his money. The Raider was now en route to St. Louis on travel orders made out to Marion Hedgepeth, paying for his meals with military vouchers made out to Marion Hedgepeth, and with Marion Hedgepeth's money in Marion Hedgepeth's wallet—all but two dollars of it.

"Oh, Andy, Andy," he said without anger, but only in sorrow. "They'll throw you in jail."

He had no desire to pretend to be a Marine, but he could hardly walk out onto the street in his underwear. He put on the Marine uniform. Except for the sleeves being about an inch too short, it was a perfect fit, including the cap.

He felt in all the pockets, just to make sure he hadn't overlooked anything, and was pleasantly surprised to find his baggage locker key in one of the buttoned-down shirt pockets. He transferred it to a jacket pocket, along with the two-dollar bill.

When Marion Hedgepeth stepped from the alley, the change in his appearance was startling. His nearly shaved head, so ludicrous under the baby blue cap, gave him an almost murderous appearance with the Marine cap perched on it. He looked every inch a warrior.

On the sidewalk he paused to glance around. No one was in sight, but to his right a brighter glow of street lights indicated a main drag. Walking to the corner, he looked around again, and got his bearings when he spotted the tavern where he had met Andy only a quarter block away. He turned in the other direction, toward the bus depot.

He had no idea what time it was, but he guessed from the small amount of traffic and the few pedestrians on the street that it must be well past midnight. He passed a couple of strolling Army privates going in the opposite direction, who looked at him with respect and a touch of awe. He didn't even see them because he was thinking about Andy.

What was he going to do about him, he wondered? He knew that what he *should* do was stop the first shore patrolman he saw and report what had happened. But that would mean wires being sent and Andy being dragged from the bus in handcuffs somewhere between Los Angeles and St. Louis, and he couldn't stand that thought. He held no resentment for what the Raider had done to him. Andy was still a hero in his eyes, and his desertion was justified. He wished Andy hadn't deserted, but now that he had, Marion would be in no way responsible for his apprehension. He was welcome to his baby blue suit, his papers, and his money, if they would keep the Marine out of jail.

He passed a couple of other uniforms without looking at them, his thoughts turned inward. Then he came to a halt when a peremptory voice said behind him, "You passed two officers, Marine!"

He did a clumsy about-face and peered at the two youthful ensigns who were glaring at him. Because he wasn't thinking of himself as a Marine, he forgot he was wearing the uniform, and was puzzled at what they wanted.

"Huh?" he said.

The ensigns took in the Raider's patch and the ribbons. They also took in the spaced-out look in his eyes, and interpreted it as combat fatigue.

"Forget it," the one who had called him said.

They turned around and walked on.

It wasn't until their backs were to him that he remembered he was in Marine uniform. *Called me Marine,* he said to himself, straightening his shoulders in sudden pride. Turning around, he strode on, now erect, his chest thrust out and his stomach pulled in.

His thoughts returned to Andy. Now that he had decided he would never turn him in, he wondered what Andy would do and where he would go. Certainly he wouldn't take the last leg of the journey authorized at government expense in the stolen orders, to Crystal City, and attempt to pass himself off there as Marion Hedgepeth, because that idea was ridiculous. Probably he would buy civilian clothing in some St. Louis secondhand shop, then just disappear.

The thought made him wonder why Andy hadn't simply walked into some Los Angeles secondhand shop to buy civilian clothes instead of going through this elaborate plot, but he immediately realized the answer. Servicemen were forbidden to wear anything but their uniforms for the duration, so the secondhand dealer would instantly know the purchaser was a deserter, and probably would call the shore patrol. Getting rid of the baby blue suit would be understandable, though.

That thought made Marion realize that even if he had the money to buy civilian clothes, he was stuck with the Marine uniform until he got home. He would have to time things to arrive in Crystal City late at night, he thought, sneak into the house, change into his civilian clothes, then sneak down to the basement to burn the Marine uniform before awakening his parents.

His thoughts broke off as he neared the taxi-dance hall a short distance from the bus depot and spotted a crowd outside of it. He slowed to see what was going on.

Apparently it was merely intermission time, and a group of taxi-dancers and servicemen had stepped outdoors for a breath of air. The center of attention was a large, brutal-looking Paratrooper sergeant with an array of combat ribbons who was holding court. The girls were regarding him with admiration, and the servicemen were laughing at what he was saying with the nervousness of mixed admiration and fear. The sergeant held a beer bottle in his hand, as did most of the other servicemen.

As Marion halted, the sergeant was just delivering the punch line of a joke. " 'Sure I guarantee the parrot's only previous owner was a preacher,' the pet store guy told the old lady. 'He was a chaplain in the Marines.' "

He roared at his own joke, the other servicemen obediently chuckled, and the girls tittered.

Chapter 7

Marion started to move on, but halted again when the Paratrooper said, "Hey! Hey! Heyyy—"

Marion gave him a look of innocent inquiry.

"Well, well, lookit here," the sergeant said. "A real live Raider Marine."

Those between the sergeant and Marion suddenly moved aside to leave an opening between them. They expected a fight, Marion realized without fear, but with sudden wariness. He had no desire to fight, not because he was afraid, but because fighting without purpose, just to be fighting, had always struck him as idiotic. He said nothing.

"I hear Raiders just can't get enough fighting," the sergeant challenged.

"When we have to," Marion said equably.

The Paratrooper drained his beer bottle, flipped it to catch the empty bottle by the neck, and swaggered over to within two feet of Marion. "Well, now's when you have to."

Marion eyed the bottle warily. Off to his right he heard a sailor say to one of the taxi-dancers, "I just love to see Guyrines get cold-cocked."

When the Paratrooper made no threatening moves with the bottle, Marion shifted his gaze from it to the man's ribbons. "Think you'd had enough fighting," he commented.

"Me? Mac, it just gave me a taste for it. So you know what we're going to do? Not Army against Marines. Paratroopers and Raiders. See, we don't have to go around wearing that shitty little ain't-I-tough patch."

Marion said, "I don't want to fight, Sergeant."

"Well, I don't blame you. Because I got to warn you about my nickname. Cement-head."

Because he had been inside dancing, the sergeant was not wearing his cap but had it folded and tucked into his belt. Marion looked without understanding at the bristly stubble of black hair covering his bullet-shaped head in a quarter-inch G.I. haircut. Then the sergeant made it understandable by very deliberately breaking the beer bottle over his own head.

He didn't even blink. A chorus of amazed and delighted sounds came from the onlookers.

Grinning ferociously, the sergeant said, "And I take off bottlecaps with my teeth."

He tossed the neck of the bottle aside. Marion braced himself for attack, but the sergeant wasn't yet through talking. He said, "But you see I got a kind of advantage, and nobody can say old Cement-head ain't fair. So how we work it is this: you get a free shot. And then I get one. And when you get up, if you do, the fight starts."

"I don't want to fight," Marion repeated.

"Well, you're goddamn going to." Bracing his feet, the Paratrooper thrust out his chin and tapped it with his finger. "Sorry about your hand."

Marion's right hand became a fist, but it remained hanging at his side.

Apparently to maintain his self-induced high, the Paratrooper suddenly said, "Damn it, I got to keep *warmed up!*" and thrust out his hand sidewise, palm up, like a surgeon requesting a scalpel from a nurse.

Someone filled it with an empty beer bottle. Again he shattered the bottle over his own head and contemptuously tossed aside the neck. He stood there like a block of granite, seemingly incapable of being damaged by anything.

Again thrusting out his chin, he said, "You don't, I will."

Marion obliged him. His large fist whistled through the air to land solidly on the button. The Paratrooper's eyes went blank. For a moment he stood still, as though trying to remember something important, such as how to stand up. Then he toppled over on his back, out cold.

Rubbing his stinging fist, Marion said to the gaping faces around him, "Trick was not to hit him on top of the head."

When Marion got to the bus depot, the first thing he did was look at the clock over the information counter. It was 12:25.

Andy was on the road nearly two hours by now, he thought. Good luck to him.

There was a different woman behind the information counter than when he came in from San Diego, he noted. She was younger and dark-haired and rather pretty in her neat gray uniform. No one happened to be at the counter at the moment. Seeing him looking at her from across the room, she smiled at him. He was rather surprised, but then he realized it was the uniform she was smiling at, not him. Nevertheless he smiled back.

At this time of night the waiting room was not very crowded. Only four civilians and about a dozen servicemen were in it. Six of the servicemen, probably all having several hours wait for their busses, were stretched out asleep on benches.

He hadn't given any thought as to where he was going to spend the night, but now it occurred to him that the bus waiting room was as good a place as any.

He went over to his luggage locker and was about to insert the key when it occurred to him that if he removed his bag, it would cost another dime to lock it up again. There was still a slight taste of vomit and stale Scotch in his mouth, and he would have liked to brush his teeth, but he decided it wasn't worth breaking his two-dollar bill.

He put the key back into his pocket, went into the washroom and thoroughly rinsed out his mouth. Then he returned to the waiting room, folded his cap, tucked it into his belt, stretched out on his back on a bench and went to sleep.

A gentle shake on the shoulder awakened him. Opening his eyes, he looked up into the apologetic face of the young woman who had been behind the information desk last night.

"Sorry to disturb you, Corporal," she said. "But you've been sleeping so long, I was afraid you might have missed your bus."

Sitting up, he glanced at the clock and saw it was 8:00 A.M. "Thank you, ma'am," he said. "I still have time."

She looked faintly puzzled. "Oh. Well, I'm going off duty, and thought I ought to check before I left."

"I appreciate it," he said, getting to his feet.

With a smiling nod, she turned and walked away. He looked around the waiting room. It was packed now, mostly with servicemen, but even at this early hour he noted a number of heavily made-up women seated with expectant expressions on their faces, and several teen-age girls he suspected were V-girls.

Going over to his locker, he got out his bag. In the washroom he washed and brushed his teeth, considered changing into his single fresh change of underwear and socks, and decided he had better save it. Putting on his hat, he examined himself in the mirror. Despite sleeping in it, his uniform was unwrinkled and still looked neat.

Carrying his bag out to the waiting room, he paused to contemplate his next move. It ought to be breakfast, he thought, because he was ravenously hungry. But with home 2,000 miles away, he felt he ought to save his two dollars for dire emergencies.

If there was a USO or Red Cross club nearby, he could probably get free coffee and donuts, he thought. He went over to the information counter, where there was now a different woman on duty. She directed him to a USO club only two blocks away, where he had five donuts and a cup of coffee.

Emerging from the club with his hunger satisfied, he considered how he was going to get home. Obviously he was going to have to hitchhike, but while by bus he had no choice of routes, hitchhiking he could take either the southern route along 66 through Arizona, New Mexico, the Texas Panhandle and Oklahoma, up into southern Missouri, or the northern route through northern California, Nevada, Utah, Wyoming, Nebraska, Iowa and Illinois, into eastern Missouri.

He decided he would leave it to chance, accepting the first ride offered in either direction. His immediate problem was to get out of town and onto the highway.

He headed for the nearest corner, planning to start thumbing from there. Just as he got there, an empty produce truck stopped for a light. On impulse he tossed his bag in back and pulled himself up over the tailgate.

Since he was unfamiliar with Los Angeles, he had no idea where the truck was taking him, but they seemed to be heading north and west. After about twenty minutes the countryside began to appear a little more open and the truck picked up speed, indicating they were on some kind of highway. Then it slowed, pulled onto a graveled parking lot and stopped.

Lifting his bag, Marion vaulted over the tailgate to the ground. Hearing the cab door slam shut, he peered around the rear of the truck to see a burly man in overalls heading for a diner situated in the center of the lot. A number of semis parked around the diner indicated the place was a truck stop.

There was a highway marker on the road shoulder just in front of the truck stop designating the road as Highway 101. At an intersection about fifty yards beyond there was a large rectangular sign giving distances. Marion walked up to look at it. It read: VENTURA—60; SANTA BARBARA —90; SAN FRANCISCO—455.

That settled the question of which route he would take, he thought. It had to be the northern route.

Holding his bag in his left hand, he began thumbing with his right. Because of gas and tire rationing there was not much traffic. Two cars passed, already loaded with servicemen the drivers had picked up farther back. A 1937 Plymouth with a woman driver went by, the woman apologetically pointing to the "A" sticker on her windshield as she passed, apparently meaning it to signal that she was only going a short distance.

Then there was no traffic for a time. Marion began to

walk along the shoulder, whistling "From the Halls of Montezuma."

Hearing a car engine behind him, he turned and put up his thumb. The car slowed and stopped alongside of him. It was a 1936 Buick sedan with a "C" sticker on the windshield. The driver was a scrawny, spectacled man of around sixty wearing blue denim trousers and a blue flannel shirt.

Smiling, Marion tossed his bag in back and climbed in the front seat. Then his smile faded as it struck him that this was going to be the first real test of his skill as an imposter.

As the car started up again, he said a trifle nervously, "Much obliged, sir."

"Anything for the Marines," the driver said. "Where to?"

"Far as you're going, sir."

"Your lucky day," the man chuckled. "Going to hell and gone." After a pause, he said, "And forget the sir. Wasn't even in the first one."

Marion started to say, "Yes, sir," but caught himself and merely nodded.

The man glanced sidewise at the death's-head shoulder patch and the ribbons on Marion's chest. "Guadalcanal?" he inquired.

His voice muffled with guilt, Marion muttered, "Raiders."

"Pardon?"

"Raiders," Marion said more distinctly.

The driver's eyes widened, and he threw another look at the death's-head shoulder patch. "Oh, my God! I read about you in *Look*. Out there on some island infested with Japs, you went ashore in rubber boats. Night. Black, with knives in your teeth, piano wire for strangling. You went in and out, like ghosts, and a hundred little yellow bastards gone to their ancestors. My God, congratulations."

Marion had not heard this particular story before. He could think of nothing to say except, "Yes, sir."

At noon they stopped at a roadside diner, and the

Buick driver insisted on buying his passenger's lunch. Marion had only a hamburger and a glass of milk.

When they continued on, they rode in silence for some time. Marion's thoughts returned to Andy, and again he wondered what would happen to him. He had no idea what the punishment for desertion was, but he suspected it would be at least several years in a federal prison. Perhaps the Buick driver knew.

He broke the lengthy silence by saying, "You know, sir, a buddy of mine's got a problem."

The older man gave him a quzzical look. "A buddy of yours?" he said in a tone suggesting he knew what was coming: the old "friend of mine" cover for a problem which was really the narrator's own problem.

Marion completely missed the intonation, mainly because it actually was a buddy he was talking about. He said, "See, I'm lucky. I'm going home, but my buddy, he went through hell with me, and they're sending him back over there. He's thinking of deserting."

The driver inhaled sharply. In a grim tone he said, "Well, I sure hope he don't."

"Yes, sir. What I told him. Could get prison."

"In wartime? Get hung."

Marion stared at him, appalled at the risk Andy had taken. "After all he's been through?"

"Hunt him down like a dog. So tell your buddy to forget it." There was a long pause, before he added earnestly, "And good luck to him."

"Yes, sir," Marion said.

He looked out the window. If there had been any question in his mind about eventually reporting what had happened, there no longer was. He would never tell on Andy.

A series of Burma Shave signs caught his eye, and he read the message on each as it flashed by. THE BEARDED DEVIL, read the first. The next three read IS FORCED TO DWELL—IN THE ONLY PLACE—WHERE THEY DON'T SELL. Then the final sign, as always, read BURMA SHAVE.

Chapter 8

The Buick took him all the way to San Francisco, and the driver bought him dinner before they parted. He also again stressed that Marion had better talk his buddy out of deserting.

Again he slept at the bus depot. In the morning he had a free breakfast and a shower at the Red Cross Service Club. He also washed out his dirty socks and underwear while under the shower. Putting on his fresh set, he walked to a nearby park and hung his wet laundry from a tree limb to dry while he lolled on a park bench.

There was a warm breeze, and by 10:00 A.M. it was dry. He stowed it in his bag, caught a ride to the edge of town, and hitchhiked on his way.

He made fair time, although not really good time. It took him two days to get to Salt Lake City, but every driver who picked him up bought him meals, and he arrived there late on a Wednesday night with his two dollars still intact.

As usual he slept at the bus depot, and the next morning hunted up the Red Cross Service Club for a free breakfast, a shower, and to wash his laundry. By 10:30 the laundry was dry and stowed in his bag.

Since he would probably never again get to Salt Lake City, he decided to take the time to see the famous Mormon Tabernacle. When he got there, he discovered a service was just going to start. It seemed that the tabernacle had daily services, not just on Sunday. His uniform got him invited to a half dozen different homes after church. He accepted the invitation of a middle-aged couple who said they had a son in the Air Force in North

Africa. He picked them over all the others, including a family with an attractive teen-age daughter, because he wouldn't be expected to know anything either about the Air Force or the situation in North Africa.

He was invited to spend the night, but in late afternoon decided he had better move on. The couple drove him to the edge of town and dropped him on the main highway going east. He got a ride almost immediately, but it took him only a few miles to a fork where the main road went northeast toward Cheyenne, and a lesser road went southeast toward Denver.

Several cars stopped for him, but they were all taking the southeast branch of the fork. When it began to near dusk, he decided he had better take the next ride offer that came along, regardless of which branch the driver was taking, or he might be stuck out there all night. Although the secondary road wasn't as well traveled, it wouldn't be any farther to go through Colorado, Kansas, and then into Missouri at Kansas City than to take the so-called main northern route.

A few minutes later a farmer in a pickup truck stopped for him. It developed he was taking the road toward Denver, and also developed that he was going only fifty miles, to a farm out in the middle of nowhere.

Marion was contemplating sleeping in some cornfield when the farmer offered to put him up overnight and feed him breakfast in the morning. The pseudo-Marine accepted with alacrity.

The farmer and his wife had no sons in service, but they went all out to make up for it by treating the Marine corporal like a son. They not only fed him and gave him a bed, but the wife insisted on doing his laundry and pressing his uniform. She gave him a robe belonging to her husband to wear while she pressed the uniform.

In the morning he borrowed shoe-shine equipment, and when he left, he was as spic-and-span as though prepared to fall in for a formal inspection.

It was some time before he got a ride, and when he did, it was another farmer in a pickup truck who was going only twenty miles. His next two rides were also short, and he had long waits in between them. By noon he had made less than one hundred miles.

He was starting to become hungry. He would have broken his two-dollar bill for a meal if he could have found a restaurant, but there were none along this road. He began looking for fruit trees, but there were none of those either. This was sheep country, with few trees, and what few he saw were shade trees around farm-houses.

He began to regret not holding out for a ride along the main road the previous evening.

He had been walking along the road shoulder for about a half hour after being dumped off by the third farmer, without a single vehicle coming along in his direction, although several passed going the other way. Then, finally, he heard a car approaching from behind him.

Stepping close to the edge of the shoulder, he held up a thumb. He had just rounded a curve, so he couldn't see the approaching vehicle until it came around the curve also, but by the sound of the engine he could tell it was a powerful car.

When it appeared around the curve, and he saw the red-lensed light on its roof, he hurriedly dropped his thumb. But it was too late. The car braked to a halt along-side of him. It was a Ford sedan with a decal on its front door reading COUNTY SHERIFF. A large, red-faced man in a khaki uniform and a flat-brimmed hat was behind the wheel.

"Hop in, Corporal," he called amiably.

With the natural reluctance of an imposter to have any contact with police, Marion stalled for time by asking, "Where to, sir?" It was his intention to politely refuse the lift, no matter where the car was bound, on the excuse that it wasn't far enough, and he might miss another ride going farther.

"Bidwell," the red-faced man said. "Not much, but you can get something to eat."

The man's tone was so friendly that Marion's apprehen-sion evaporated. Besides it suddenly occurred to him that refusing a ride might make the man suspicious. Smiling appreciation, he climbed into the front seat next to the driver and dropped his bag between his feet.

As the car started to move, Marion took in the pump shotgun in a bracket just in front of him, and the holstered .45 revolver hanging from the red-faced man's belt. At the same time the driver was taking in the Raider patch and the combat ribbons.

"Jim Wenzel," the driver said. "Sheriff."

"Marion Hedgepeth. Corporal."

Marion hadn't meant it to be funny, but the sheriff chuckled in appreciation of his wit. "Denver?"

"Yes, sir. Then St. Louis. Kind of seeing the country."

With another glance at the ribbons, Sheriff Wenzel said, "Looks like you've already seen a lot."

"Enough to last," Marion said briefly, hoping his tone would close that subject.

It did. There was considerable silence before the sheriff finally threw him another side-glance and said, "Excuse me, but I don't recognize that outfit patch."

"Raiders," Marion said. "Maybe you've heard of us."

The sheriff examined him with a mixture of surprise and awe. "I've heard of you," he affirmed. After long silence, he said hesitantly, "Just say if I'm out of line, and I know about military secrets, but are we doing all right out there?"

"Yes, sir," Marion said with the confidence of complete ignorance. "We'll beat 'em."

Sheriff Wenzel looked pleased. After a time he said, "Think they'd give a fellow like you a plane ride home. Sooner be with his folks."

Marion's growing confidence in the success of his masquerade evaporated. It was the sort of comment he dreaded, because it required on-the-spot invention in order to avert suspicion.

With the barest hesitation he thought of a plausible explanation. "No family to speak of. Hardly knew my dad, and mother's dead." *Mom and Dad forgive me,* he thought.

The sheriff gave him a sympathetic look. "And then you got to fight, too."

As that seemed to require no answer, Marion made none.

The road had been steadily climbing. Now it leveled off on what seemed to be a plateau. The land was harsher here, and the few trees scrubbier in this higher country. The area had once been forested, it was obvious from the row after row of stumps reaching to the horizon, but all except the scrubby trees had long since been cut down. For miles there was no sign of habitation, and even no sign of the sheep that had been in plentiful evidence only a few miles farther west.

Ahead and off to the left, some distance back from the highway, Marion glimpsed a high barbwire fence beyond which were the silhouettes of low buildings with corrugated iron roofs. As they drew nearer, he saw that it was a sizable settlement, virtually a small town, completely surrounded by barbwire.

The sheriff seemed acutely conscious of his passenger staring toward the settlement. He didn't even glance that way himself, and his sudden over-heartiness when he spoke suggested he was attempting to divert Marion's attention from the place.

"Bidwell just a mile," he said. "Yes, sir, Oasis Café. Get a nice thick steak there with all the trimmings, apple pie and——"

"What's that?" Marion broke in, gazing at the huge barbwire enclosure, now directly alongside of them.

Sheriff Wenzel threw a glance that way, as though just noticing the place. In an offhand voice he said, "Government land. Used to be an old logging camp."

The car speeded up, reached the edge of the plateau, and started down a steep hill into a wide valley.

"Barbwire?" Marion said curiously. "Is that Army?"

Trapped into a direct answer, the sheriff emitted a sigh and said, "Japs."

"Japs?" Marion repeated in surprise.

Apparently the sheriff assumed the word would enrage his Raider passenger, because he said in a placating tone, "Not real Japs, understand. American ones." There was a pause before he explained, "Guess when you're *in* the war, it's hard to know what's going on back home. You see, son, after Pearl Harbor it got scary."

The internment program, Marion realized. He had read of how early the previous year the government had moved all Japanese from the West Coast to relocation camps farther inland, and that one of them was in Colorado. There had been considerable controversy over the program, with some Senators and Congressmen violently opposing it. But in the end both the President and Congress had bowed to the overwhelming public belief that no Japanese could be trusted.

Marion himself had mixed feelings about the program. While he tended to subscribe to the widespread belief that no alien Jap could be trusted, nearly two-thirds of the internees were nisei, or American-born Japanese, and he was a little dubious about American citizens, even yellow ones, being uprooted from their homes and thrown into concentration camps. He had no really strong feelings about the matter either way, however.

He said, "Read about it. Afraid of invasion, spies."

Sheriff Wenzel seemed relieved at the Marine corporal's mild reaction. He said, "Well, there was no invasion, but don't let anybody tell you there wasn't spies." After a pause he said, "Los Angeles Japs in there. Army guards, so we don't have anything to do with 'em."

"Ever have any trouble?"

The sheriff considered this before saying with curious reluctance, "Three in there. Hell-raisers. Mean. Nailed 'em breaking out a while back."

When his passenger failed to ask for any details, he added, "The others stay in line. Hard-working little people. They say that about Japs."

When Marion still made no comment, the sheriff said even more reluctantly, and with a strange air of defiance, as though expecting disagreement, but determined to express his opinion anyway, "Wouldn't want you to get me wrong. I'm no Jap-lover, but most of 'em were born here."

Marion made no comment to that either. After waiting

in vain for one for several seconds, the sheriff said rather lamely, "But like they say, remember Pearl Harbor."

"Yes, sir," Marion said. "That's right."

Chapter 9

As the sheriff's car descended the hill, they got a bird's-eye view of the village at the bottom of the hill. The highway bisected it, becoming the main street as it passed through town. It was the only paved street. Three graveled streets ran off of it to either side, but they ran only one block in each direction, ending in other graveled streets running parallel to the main street. There were perhaps seventy-five frame houses, most of them two stories high, a few of them three, most painted white with green trim, and most looking well-kept-up. A few had trees in their yards, but no trees lined the streets, as they did in Marion's home town. The spires of two churches on opposite sides of the street graced either end of town. The business section was the central block of town, where stores and other business establishments lined both sides of the street.

At the bottom of the hill they passed a sign reading BIDWELL—POP. 317. Immediately beyond it was a sign reading SPEED LIMIT—25. Sheriff Wenzel had already slowed, and he slowed even more when they came to a second sign at the beginning of the business section lowering the speed limit to 15.

At that speed Marion had ample time to take in the view. There was a hardware store to their right, across from the Cherokee Gas Station and Repair Garage. The Hotel Astoria occupied the second floor of a building, above a barbershop and a combination dry-goods store and drugstore, the hotel's entrance being between them. Directly across from it was the Granada Theater. Next to the barbershop was a shoe repair shop, and across from it a small grocery store. A restaurant was beyond the shoe repair shop, on the right side of the street at the end of the block. Across from it was a small, one-story frame building.

The sheriff swung left across the street to park diagonally in front of the small building. Marion saw that a sign above its door read SHERIFF'S SUB-STATION.

They got out of the car. Nodding toward the restaurant across the street, Sheriff Wenzel said, "Oasis Café, the hub of Bidwell's social life. Opens at five A.M. for the railroad men, closes at eight P.M. In between, you can get milkshakes and coffee and the best roast beef sandwiches with country gravy in the county."

"Maybe I'll try it," Marion said. "Thanks for the ride, sir."

"You're welcome, son."

The sheriff went into the sub-station. Marion crossed the street. The Oasis Café was a small, square, one-story building surrounded by a graveled parking lot. Only a pickup truck and two cars were parked on the lot. Marion hesitated on the sidewalk in front of the place for a time, weighing whether to hitchhike on and hope whoever picked him up hadn't yet lunched, or finally to break his two-dollar bill. Hunger won out.

The inside of the café was sparkling clean but had about as much atmosphere as a chain drugstore snack bar. There were booths along the front wall and one side. Twin counters formed a right angle, with an opening next to the cash register to permit booth service. There was a cigarette machine and a jukebox. A curling strip of flypaper hung from the center of the ceiling.

There were only four customers. A skinny, pimply-faced Army private of about eighteen sat in a booth, eating a piece of pie à la mode and reading a comic book. At the counter parallel to the front door three men wearing blue-and-white striped railroad shirts, overalls and brakemen's caps dawdled over heavy mugs of coffee.

Marion seated himself at the other counter, which faced the service counter into the kitchen. Through the opening he could see a slightly overweight man of about forty with a round, good-natured face, dressed in a white tee-shirt, white apron and a white chef's cap. He set his bag on the floor next to his feet.

Marion grew conscious of becoming the center of attention of the other four customers. From across the room the Army private was examining him with a mixture of envy and faint antagonism. The three railroad men gazed at him. Two, both in their mid-forties, merely regarded him with friendly interest. But the one in the center, a heavy-featured and heavy-shouldered man in his early fifties, stared at him with an intentness that made Marion uneasy. He smiled at all three men, but only two smiled back. The heavy-shouldered man continued to stare at him without expression.

The door from the kitchen opened and a waitress stepped out, smiling over her shoulder at something said by the cook. Then she turned, her eyes met Marion's, and she stopped dead still.

Marion had the sensation that rockets were going off all around him. Gradually, as he began to regain his senses, he realized to his utter astonishment that she was looking at him as though seeing and hearing invisible rockets too.

She was the loveliest thing he had ever seen in his nearly nineteen years. About eighteen, she had a slim, trim figure encased in a red-and-white checked gingham uniform with pockets and buttons down the front. She had chestnut hair curling to her shoulders, delicate features, a smooth, glowing complexion, and a look of utter innocence.

They stared at each other in mutual certainty that IT had happened. The girl was first to recover.

"Afternoon," she said in a husky tone that curled his toes.

"Hi," he managed.

Rapidly, looking directly into his eyes as she spoke, and reciting as though it were merely something to be gotten out of the way before they got to more important matters, she said, "Special's roast beef with mashed potatoes, including soup, salad, pie or cake, and beverage of your choice."

Food had suddenly become unimportant to Marion. Besides, he was going to need his two dollars to squander on the girl. He couldn't very well just sit there without ordering anything, though. He decided to spend a nickel.

"Just coffee," he said, at the same moment she opened her mouth to say more. "Oh, excuse me for interrupting."

Apparently she decided that whatever she had planned to say was unnecessary if he didn't intend to eat, because she merely nodded and went over to the urn to draw a cup of coffee.

Conscious that he was staring at her shapely back and equally shapely legs in what onlookers might construe as a lascivious manner, he wrenched his gaze away and threw a quick checking glance around at the others in the room.

The private in the booth was now literally glaring, his gaze jumping back and forth from Marion to the girl. It was not hard to deduce that he had a crush on the girl, had sensed her instant impact on the Marine corporal, his equally instant impact on her, and hated them both for it.

The three railroad men were still looking at him also, but their expressions were unchanged. The two younger ones still showed only friendly interest, and the heavy-shouldered man between them continued to gaze at him unblinkingly. By now Marion had come to the conclusion that there was neither suspicion nor hostility in the steady gaze. He had the peculiar impression that it somehow represented controlled grief.

The girl set the mug before him, with a small individual cream server and a sugar dispenser. He gave a smiling shake of the head to indicate that he used neither, wrapped both hands about the mug and took a cautious sip.

The girl examined the salt and pepper shakers in front of Marion. Both were two-thirds full, but she picked them up and carried them to the back counter for refilling anyway. As she refilled them, the heavy-shouldered railroad man transferred his attention to her and made a motion indicating he wanted her to come over.

The waitress replaced the shakers in front of Marion before going over to see what the man wanted. He said something in such a low voice that she had to bend her head toward him and ask him to repeat it. She nodded and returned to Marion.

"We serve breakfast all hours," she said. "Eggs, ham, home fries—" She let it trail off.

"Coffee's just fine, thank you," he said.

She threw an uncertain glance at the railroad man. He nodded, just once, rather curtly.

Turning back to Marion, she said with a touch of embarrassment, "You don't need money. Mr. Elmore would consider it an honor."

Frowning, Marion looked toward the heavy-shouldered man. He was still expressionless, but his two companions were both looking sidewise at him with sympathetic sadness. Marion got it then, and it made him feel terrible. Up to now his imposture had merely been a necessary deceit to get himself home. But suddenly it was deceiving a grieving father. He wished devoutly he was a real Marine, so that the man's gesture in memory of his lost son would not ring so hollow.

But he couldn't refuse the offer, because the unkindness would be worse than the sham. Besides, he *was* hungry.

He said, "Thank you very much, sir."

The man gave him a bare nod, then looked down into his coffee cup. Marion said to the girl, "Believe ham 'n eggs *would* be good."

She turned her head to call over her shoulder, "Ham and, Charlie."

The round-faced cook had been standing facing Marion from inside the kitchen, waiting for a decision. He immediately set to work. The girl made out a check, set it in front of Mr. Elmore, then set water, silverware and a paper napkin in front of Marion.

Attempting to be casual, Marion said, "Nice little town."

The girl carefully repositioned the salt and pepper shakers. "Just passing through," she said. It was a statement, not a question.

He said, "Denver."

She gave him a wistful smile. "I've been to Denver twice."

He nodded, trying to think of something else to say, something brilliant and witty that would make her laugh. Then he remembered he was still wearing his cap, took it off to put it on the counter, and knocked over the pepper shaker.

He flamed red at his awkwardness, but she only smiled, righted the shaker and quickly wiped away the spilled grains with a damp cloth.

"Lucky it wasn't the salt," she said cheerfully.

"Right," he said, grateful for her turning it into a small joke.

He tried to think of something else to say, but his mind was a total blank. Then, gazing at her cow-eyed, he was horrified to hear himself blurting aloud what he meant merely as a silent thought. "Your hair's pretty."

She turned crimson. Quickly lifting his cup, she said, "Freshen it up," and turned her back to go to the urn.

She hadn't been offended by his freshness, he thought, relieved. She had liked the compliment.

At that moment the three men at the other counter rose from their stools and came over to the register. Apparently they all had tabs at the restaurant, because they merely put their checks on the counter and moved on toward the door. Marion saw that all three checks had signatures on them.

As the one the waitress had designated as Mr. Elmore went past him, Marion said, "Much obliged again, sir."

The man merely nodded again, a single, immensely dignified nod.

As the three men went out the door, the girl called after them brightly, "Come on back and see us, now."

The two younger men grinned back at her over their shoulders. Mr. Elmore gave no sign that he had even heard.

©Lorillard 1975
Come for the filter...
A PRODUCT OF
Lorillard
KENT
WITH
THE FAMOUS MICRONITE FILTER
DELUXE LENGTH
Warning: The Surgeon General Has Determined That Cigarette Smoking Is Dangerous to Your Health.
18 mg. "tar," 1.2 mg. nicotine av. per cigarette, FTC Report Oct. '74.

©Lorillard 1975
...you'll stay for the taste.
DELUXE LENGTH
KENT
WITH THE FAMOUS MICRONITE FILTER
A lot of good taste that comes easy through the Micronite filter.
18 mg. "tar," 1.2 mg. nicotine av. per cigarette, FTC Report Oct. '74.
Warning: The Surgeon General Has Determined That Cigarette Smoking Is Dangerous to Your Health.

Chapter 10

The cook slid a steaming platter onto the service counter and called, "Ham and!"

The girl turned to lift down the platter and set it before Marion. He stared down at the three large sunnyside eggs, huge slab of grilled ham, fried potatoes and toast.

"Enough for an army," he commented.

"Or one Marine," she said lightly.

They smiled at each other. He reached for the salt, still looking at her, dropped the shaker and spilled a small amount of salt on the counter. This time he wasn't even embarrassed, though. Grinning, he picked up a pinch and threw it over his shoulder before righting the shaker. She wiped up the rest of the spilled salt with the wet cloth.

He picked up the shaker again, this time more carefully, and began to salt his food. Then he stopped to look up at her.

"Awful nice of that man," he said.

She looked past him through the front windows to the parking lot, where a car was just pulling out. "Mr. Elmore's a brakeman on the railroad," she said. "The S.P. He lost his boy at Pearl Harbor."

He had known it was something like that. He said, "Oh, I'm sorry."

"Johnny was the best football player Riverton ever had. Riverton's where I graduated from. *Was* graduated from, I mean. My dad teaches Latin there." She looked down at the platter. "Hey, it'll get cold."

The salt shaker was still suspended over the platter. He resumed shaking, added some pepper, and began to eat. The girl busied herself with some meaningless work nearby, rinsing out the wet cloth, stacking some napkins, checking the sugar dispensers.

"From Denver?" she asked.

He shook his head. "Just seeing a bit of the country. Little town outside of St. Louis you never heard of." He chewed and swallowed a piece of ham before adding, "My name's Marion Hedgepeth."

In a shy voice she said, "Rose Hudkins."

"Pleased to meet you," he said, smiling. "Rose is nice." He took a bite of potatoes, chewed and swallowed before appending reflectively, "Marion's kind of a girl's name."

"Well, I bet nobody's dumb enough to say so," she said with the obvious conviction that anyone that dumb would be courting danger. "What do they call you?"

All his life Marion had secretly longed for a particular nickname. But all his friends had called him Marion. "Hedge," he said.

"I like that," she said in a pleased tone. "Okay, Hedge."

She watched him eat for a few moments. Her gaze touched his ribbons, then, for the first time, she noticed his death's-head shoulder patch.

"That's kind of scary," she said.

He looked up, saw her examining the patch, and said embarrassedly, "Don't have to be afraid of me."

She looked him over thoroughly, including his nearly bald head, before saying reflectively, "You know, you're different than what I expected."

"Oh?" he said with a touch of uneasiness.

"I mean a Marine like *you* coming here is like General MacArthur walking in." She indicated his ribbons. "All the battles you've been in."

He concentrated on his plate, mute with guilt. She instantly sensed that she had disturbed him, but she came nowhere near guessing why.

"Oh, I'm sorry, Hedge," she said contritely. "I don't mean to have you talk about it."

"It's okay, Rose."

But he had lost his appetite. He had already eaten two of the eggs and about half of the ham and potatoes. He began to push the rest about on his plate as he gazed down at it, his thoughts on the disgrace that lay ahead of him when he got home. After a time he looked up, gazed out the front windows and sighed.

"Seems like everything's bad everywhere else. Wish I could stay here."

She stopped breathing. She couldn't breath, for hope. "You know people in Denver?" she asked.

He turned back to look at her. "Just passing through, like here."

Almost coming apart, she said, "Well, you know, I mean——"

A voice from almost next to Marion interrupted her and startled both of them. "Rose?"

Both swung sidewise. The Army private stood there, holding out a dollar bill. He said, "Apple à la mode and coffee." The rolled up comic book was clenched in his left hand.

"Oh, yes, Danny." Taking her order book from her pocket, she quickly wrote a ticket and accepted the dollar. "Danny, meet Corporal Hedgepeth. Hedge, Danny Phelps."

"Hi," Marion said.

The envy and antagonism were patent in the private's curt, "What say?"

Rose rang the cash register and handed Private Phelps his change. Danny was examining Marion's ribbons.

"Danny's just back from basic," Rose said.

"Yeah," the boy said. "Going into tanks."

In a puzzled tone Rose said, "Your mother said typing school. Said they were going to make you a corporal clerk."

Through his teeth Danny said, "She don't know nothing about it." Turning back to Marion, he said with offhand bravery, "Eighty percent casualties in tanks."

Hiking his eyebrows, Marion made a sympathetic noise. Pocketing his change, the Army private plucked a toothpick from the cut-glass holder next to the cash register and popped it into his mouth at an arrogant angle. "See you later, Rose," he said, and headed for the door.

He paused there, to turn in afterthought and say to

Marion in a tone that made the words a lie, "Nice meeting you."

"Same here," Marion said. "Good luck, Army."

He went out, leaving Marion and Rose all alone. In the kitchen the cook could be heard banging pots out of their sight. The two looked at each other, and Rose returned to the matter Private Phelps had interrupted. "When you said it was so nice here—" She let it trail off.

"Sure is," he agreed.

"But you're in a hurry to get on to Denver."

He realized she was asking him to stay over. He so badly wanted to that he was momentarily unable to speak. The silence killed her eager smile and she paled slightly.

He managed to get out, "Well, I *was* in a hurry, until I had this kind of cooking."

Her color returned and she looked absolutely radiant.

He said, "You know, I seemed to see a hotel sign up the street."

"The Astoria?" she said with a giggle. "We call it Bedbug Heaven. They get the railroad track crew when it works through here, an occasional drummer, once in a while some poor travelers who don't know any better."

"Where then?" he asked.

"We've got room," she said eagerly. She glanced over her shoulder, then went over to the service counter to peer into the kitchen to see if the cook was out of earshot. Returning, she leaned forward to whisper, "My mom's cooking makes him seem like Ptomaine Pete." Straightening, she said more audibly, "And the Astoria charges."

Two dollars, he thought. Even if his food and lodging were free, how could he court a girl on two dollars?

She said, "And my dad's so nice, and my brother Barney, he's thirteen. Oh, Hedge—" It was a plea.

"But just walking in," he protested. "I mean, are you sure?"

"They'd be mad if I *didn't* ask you."

He gave in. "I'd like to stay, Rose."

Having won her point by virtually throwing herself at him, she immediately underwent a transformation designed to show him that she was not the sort of girl who threw herself at boys. With no decrease in friendliness, she suddenly become a cool and poised young lady who had deigned to grant him a date in place of the teenager who a moment before had been desperately scrabbling for one.

Glancing up at the Coca-Cola clock on the wall, she said in a cool tone that somehow subtly managed to get across that while she thoroughly enjoyed talking to him, she now had duties to perform, "Thelma comes in at six and does dinner."

He looked at the clock too, seeing that it was 2:40 P.M. Humbly accepting his temporary dismissal, he said, "I could go bowling."

She shook her head. "Bowling's in Riverton, eight miles."

He pursed his lips. "Saw a movie up the street."

She shook her head again. "Open just tomorrow and Sundays." Then her face brightened as she had an idea. Gesturing toward the kitchen, she said, "Hey, Charlie always keep a pole back there. Nice trout, and the river's just over there." She pointed in a northwesterly direction.

He made a face indicating no interest in fishing. Rising from his stool, he felt in his pocket and brought out the two-dollar bill.

"Just see the sights, I guess," he said. "Be back here by six. Okay?" He picked up his cap and put it on.

"I'll be waiting," she said with a smile.

Bending over, he lifted the little canvas bag that had been sitting on the floor at his feet. "Okay to leave this here?"

"Sure," she said. "I'll take care of it."

She reached across the counter to take it from his hand and set it beneath the counter. When she straightened again, he held out the two-dollar bill.

"Can I please have change?"

"It's on Mr. Elmore's bill," she said, making no move to take the money.

"I know. I still want change."

Shrugging, she accepted the bill, punched the NO SALE button on the register, and exchanged the bill for a one, a half dollar, a quarter, two dimes and a nickel. Setting it before him, she asked, "That okay?"

"Just right," he said, putting down a dime tip and pocketing the rest.

She grinned and made a face and pushed it back toward him.

Grinning back, he said, "Just as much as you'd get from John D. Rockefeller."

He moved toward the door.

She looked at the dime, grinned again and picked it up to drop it in her pocket. "Come on back and see us now," she called, but only the words were the same as she had called to the three railroad men. The tone was totally different.

Outside Marion paused to look around. No one at all was on the street. Aside from the sheriff's car, still parked in front of the sub-station, only two other cars were in sight, both parked diagonally in front of the little grocery store next to the sub-station.

Sightseeing Bidwell wasn't going to take him until six o'clock, he thought ruefully, but he might as well kill a little time looking it over.

He strolled past the shoe repair shop, peering through the front window as he went by. A wizened little man resembling a gnome was stitching the sole of a shoe with a machine.

Gold-leaf lettering on the plate-glass window next door designated the establishment as the BON TON BARBER SHOP. The door was standing open, and Marion glanced in as he went by. It was a one-chair shop, without customers at the moment. The barber was standing in front of the mirror, shaving himself with a straight razor.

Marion stopped to read a block-lettered sign on white paper that had been taped to the inside of the glass just below the gold-leaf lettering. It read: JAPS SHAVED FREE. NOT RESPONSIBLE FOR ACCIDENTS.

Conscious of someone watching him, Marion glanced up to see the barber standing in the open doorway regarding him with curiosity. The man was about forty-five, big but soft-looking, with a puffy body and a puffy face lined with the broken red veins of a heavy drinker. One side of his face was freshly shaved, the other side was still covered with lather. Smiling at Marion, he lifted his straight razor in salute.

Ordinarily Marion was not given to snap judgments, but he instinctively disliked this man on sight. Perhaps it was because the smile never reached the barber's eyes, perhaps because there was a hint of smart-aleckness in his expression, or maybe merely because he resembled someone in Marion's forgotten past who had done him some kind of wrong. In any event, Marion had no desire to linger and have conversation with the man. Raising his right hand, palm out, in a brief return salute, he moved on.

He went past the stairway leading upward to the Astoria Hotel on the second floor, and looked in the window of the combination dry-goods store and drugstore just beyond it. Aside from some old-fashioned jars of colored water, there was nothing in the window to interest him. The window of the hardware store next door was equally uninteresting.

That was the end of the business section on that side of the street. Crossing over, he bypassed the Cherokee Gas Station and Repair Garage and paused to read the posters on the bulletin board of the Granada Theater. Both the NOW PLAYING poster and the COMING ATTRACTIONS poster billed only single pictures instead of double-features he noted, although each billed a half dozen shorts also, ranging from cartoons to Pathe News. The NOW PLAYING POSTER advertised *China,* starring Loretta Young and Alan Ladd, the COMING ATTRACTION was Bette Davis and George Brent in *Dark Victory*.

Then he noticed the dates on both posters and realized *China* had played last week, and *Dark Victory* was scheduled for this weekend. Apparently the management didn't bother to change posters until the theater opened on the weekend.

He went over to the closed box office to look at the posted prices on a sign next to the cashier's cage. The sign read: ADULTS—25¢; CHILDREN AND SERVICEMEN—15¢.

He could afford that, if he was still around tomorrow night, he thought. Only 40 cents to get the two of them in.

He moved on to the grocery store, peered through the window there and spotted a wall clock. It said ten minutes to three, which meant he still had more than three hours to kill. He continued on past the sheriff's sub-station to the end of the block, turned left along the gravel street and followed the one block to its end, turned left again and walked along that gravel street until he came to a path leading off to the right into the country-side. As it led in the general direction that Rose had said he would find the river, he took it.

Chapter 11

As the front door of the Oasis Café closed behind the departing Marine corporal, the cook came over to the service counter and peered out at Rose.

"Nice-looking boy," he commented.

"Yes," she agreed.

"Two of you seemed to be getting on real good. Surprised he took off so quick."

She colored slightly. "He's coming back at six."

"When you get off?" He grinned at her. "You must of gotten on even better'n I thought."

"He's staying overnight at our house."

"Well, well," he said. "You got on a *lot* better'n I thought."

Her color increased. "Oh, Charlie, don't try to make more of it than there is. It's just Hudkins hospitality. My folks would expect me to invite a visiting combat veteran to dinner."

"Oh, dinner too, eh?"

"Of course," she said. "Which reminds me, I better phone Mom to tell her we're having a guest."

She lifted the phone next to the cash register and called her home. After a short wait, she said, "Mom, I'm bringing a serviceman home for dinner and to spend the night."

She listened, then said with amused scorn, "Of course not Danny Phelps. This is a Marine corporal back from overseas, just passing through town. Name of Marion Hedgepeth, but he's called Hedge."

She listened again, then said, "About the same age as me. From a little town in Missouri. And do me a favor,

Mom. Make Barney clean up a little and put on some decent clothes in place of those worn-out old Levis."

After another pause, she said, "Okay. See you about six-fifteen."

Hanging up, she turned to look through the opening into the kitchen at Charlie. He was grinning at her. He began whistling "The Wedding March."

"Oh, stop it, Charlie," she said, blushing again. "I just met the boy. Go start fixing your dinner special."

"Yeah," he said, looking across at the Coca-Cola clock. "Guess I better. Gonna be Spanish meatloaf."

He disappeared back into the interior of the kitchen. Rose started to do her back-up work, filling juice glasses for her six-o'clock replacement, filling a butter tray, making a fresh urn of coffee.

The front door opened, and the heavy-shouldered brakeman who had bought the corporal's ham and eggs came in alone. His gaze swept the room, and there was a flicker of disappointment in his eyes when he saw the place was empty except for Rose.

Coming over to the counter, he took out his wallet. "How much, Rose?"

It was a transparently phony excuse for his return, she realized with sympathy. In a gentle voice she said, "Mr. Elmore, you don't pay till the end of the month."

Recognizing that she saw through his excuse, he made no effort to push it or to further disguise his reason for returning. Putting away the billfold, he took a seat at the counter and rested his elbows on the counter with his hands clasped in front of him.

"I see he's gone," he said glumly.

"Oh, no. Just seeing the sights."

There was a flicker of hope in the man's eyes. "He's staying?"

"Having dinner with us," she said a trifle shyly.

The flicker of hope died. He had come back not just to see Hedge, she realized, but to invite him to dinner at his house.

"Guess he'll go tomorrow," he said,

"I guess," she said, feeling sorry for him, but not

enough to change plans and let Hedge go to his house instead of to hers.

Elmore was silent for a time, then finally said, "Long way from home, is he?"

"Little town near St. Louis. Coffee? It's fresh made."

He shook his head. She wanted to finish her side work before any more customers came in, but sensing he wanted to talk, she stood there waiting.

"Tell his name?" he asked.

"Marion Hedgepeth. Likes to be called Hedge."

"Hedge," Elmore said, savoring the name. "Family?"

Rose was slightly embarrassed that she hadn't even asked Hedge about that. "Suppose," she said briefly.

Elmore sat in brooding silence for some moments, then reluctantly veered to a totally different subject. "Your dad says you'll be taking up nursing in the spring."

She nodded. "Still work part-time here."

"Nursing's a fine calling," he said heavily.

"Well, you never run out of sick people," she said lightly, then, when it struck her that he might construe it as a rather unfeeling remark, immediately added, "Oh, I didn't mean it that way."

He seemed not to have heard. He gazed unseeingly past her shoulder. In a faraway voice he said. "I remember when you were baptized."

Slightly embarrassed, she said, "I sure don't."

"And your first long dress."

She made a face. "Oh, I remember *that.*" She had loved it at the time, but from the sophisticated perspective of age eighteen, it seemed like a baby dress in retrospect.

He had drifted back in time. Speaking more to himself than to her, he said, "Johnny said to me, 'Dad, after the game today I saw Rose Hudkins in a green dress.' "

Now acutely embarrassed, she averted her gaze from the suffering in his face. Gradually he returned to reality. Straightening his heavy shoulders, he gave her an apologetic look. When she smiled understandingly, he made a dismissing gesture tacitly asking her to forget his momentary sentimentality.

"Hedge seems to be a nice young man," he said.

She nodded with certainty.

"They say more than anything else, boys in service like to get mail."

Puzzled by this seeming non sequitur, she said, "I guess so."

"Would you want to correspond?"

Understanding, she said, "We haven't talked about it."

Unclasping his hands, he laid them palm down on the counter and pushed himself to his feet heavily. Rather slowly he moved to the door. After pushing open the door, he turned to look back.

He said in an almost formal tone, "If you should write, Rose, please include the best personal regards of Mrs. Elmore and myself."

"Of course, Mr. Elmore."

He went on out. Through the window she watched him climb into his car, her heart almost breaking with sympathetic grief for him.

Marion followed the path for some hundred yards as it wound through the stunted undergrowth. Finally he spotted a row of small trees, which he guessed lined the bank of the river. His guess was right, he discovered moments later, when the path led him to the riverbank.

For one who had grown up only a couple of miles from the Mississippi and had learned to swim in its muddy waters, the designation "river" seemed a little flamboyant for this stream. In Missouri it would have been called a creek, because it was only about fifteen yards across at this particular point.

It was a beautiful stream though. The crystal-clear water rushed along between grassy, tree-lined banks at what he judged by the speed of a floating twig must be at least double, or perhaps even triple, the four-mile-an-hour current of the sluggish Mississippi. Probably full of mammoth trout, he thought, briefly regretting his refusal of the cook Charlie's fishing pole.

The water rushed by with only a faint murmur between the steep, straight banks, but from upstream, off to his left, he could hear the muted roar of rapids some distance away. As the path continued along the riverbank in that direction, he followed it.

The trees along the bank thinned, the banks became less steep, and the roar increased as he drew nearer to the rapids. When he finally reached them, the stream had widened to thirty yards and the banks were no more than six inches above the rushing water.

He came on the rapids suddenly, from around a bend in the stream, and stopped spellbound at the unexpected beauty of the scene. The water tumbled and bubbled around and over hundreds of boulders of various size, shooting small geysers of spray in all directions. The far bank was blanketed with yellow flowers which the sunshine made glow like eighteen-carat gold. And while the sound of the tumbling water was louder here right next to the rapids, somehow its timbre had changed from a roar to a bellowing song.

The boulder-strewn area extended for perhaps fifty yards upstream. When he had recovered from the stark beauty of the place, Marion continued on. About in the center of the rapids he came to a line of large boulders extending at fairly close intervals clear across the stream from bank to bank, like stepping-stones. A couple near the center were low enough to be wet with spray, although their tops were a foot or more above the water, but most were high enough for their upper surfaces to be completely dry.

They *were* stepping-stones, he saw, when he noticed that the path ended at the bank directly in front of the nearest stone, and continued on the other side.

He was contemplating risking the rather precarious crossing when a small movement on the other bank, a few yards left of the path, caught his eye. Shifting his gaze that way, he saw a woodchuck seated on its haunches at the very edge of the bank, staring at him. Apparently he had interrupted it in the middle of getting a drink.

Man and animal stared at each other in mutual trepidation, the woodchuck afraid because all wild animals have become conditioned to fear man, Marion afraid that if he made the slightest move, the little animal would bolt in panic. He stood stock still, thoroughly enjoying the sight of the stubby little fellow, and hoping the moment would stretch at least a bit.

It did. After a time the woodchuck seemed to decide this particular human constituted no immediate threat. Dropping to all fours, it dipped its head over the edge of the bank and finished having its drink. Then it looked up at Marion for a moment more, turned and waddled away into the underbrush.

When the animal had disappeared, Marion released his held breath and contemplated the natural bridge again. He decided to risk crossing it. It was a little scary, but not particularly difficult. He made it to the other side with only a few drops of water splashing onto his highly polished shoes.

The path continued on upstream on that side also, becoming steadily steeper. The stream narrowed again as he climbed alongside it, and again the banks became higher above the water.

After a time he paused to rest. Above and ahead about twenty yards the path looked as though it crested. He was considering whether or not to bother climbing that last twenty yards to see what was at the top when from some distance away in that direction came the sound of a bugle blowing *"Retreat."*

That decided him. Climbing the last short distance, he topped the crest onto the edge of the plateau just as the measured roll of muffled drums began to follow the last notes of the bugle call.

Only fifty yards away was the high barbwire fence enclosing the Japanese relocation camp. Just beyond the barbwire, in what resembled a company street between two rows of the tin-roofed huts, was a tall flagpole from which the American flag was being lowered. A platoon of American soldiers with rifles were presenting arms, but a middle-aged Japanese man in denim fatigues was lowering the flag. The bugler, now standing at rigid attention with his bugle tucked under his arm, was a young Japanese boy in a Boy Scout uniform. The drum corps, consisting of six drummers, was all Japanese Boy Scouts too.

A witnessing audience of Japanese, men and women of all ages, plus an assortment of children, stood at attention, giving the traditional civilian salute, holding the right hand over the heart.

Snapping to attention, Marion saluted the descending flag. As he held the salute, he noticed three young Japanese of about his age near the closest corner of the fence, well apart from everyone else. They stood with their arms folded, backs to the flag, defiantly making a production of their refusal to salute.

Must be those three hard-core nisei Sheriff Wenzel had mentioned, Marion thought, disapproving of their brazen rebellion.

Chapter 12

In downtown Los Angeles, First Street and Weller formed a narrow V as they came together at Los Angeles Street. The first blocks east of Los Angeles Street on both First and Weller were lined with Japanese restaurants and curio shops. The two-block area was known as the Japanese section.

Actually the section was almost entirely commercial. While a few merchants lived above their shops in the so-called Japanese section, there was really no specific residential area of Los Angeles where Japanese were concentrated. For the most part they were integrated in ordinary neighborhoods.

Tommy Masamura, Joe Harukawa and Jimmy Katsu, for instance, all lived in different neighborhoods of the Boyle Heights District, and attended Boyle Heights High School together.

On Sunday, December 7, 1941, the three were cruising the Japanese section on foot in the hope of running into some Japanese girls Americanized enough not to be offended by pickup attempts. When it approached noon without them scoring, they stopped for a snack of Japanese food at one of the sidewalk stands.

All three were seventeen-year-olds of less than average height, all with their coal-black hair worn in ducktail style. But aside from that, they were physically quite different. Tommy Masamura was lean to the point of thinness, Joe Harukawa was just short of plumpness, and Jimmy Katsu had the squat, powerfully muscled build of a wrestler.

It was a warm day, even though it was December, and they wore no jackets. They wore peg-top, narrow-cuffed slacks and colorful Hawaiian shirts with the tails hanging out.

A nearby radio was playing music. Suddenly the music cut off in the middle of a record and the voice of an announcer said:

> *We interrupt this program for a special news bulletin. About an hour and a half ago, at 7:55* A.M. *Honolulu time, which was 10:45* A.M. *local time, Japanese bombers attacked the United States naval facility at Pearl Harbor. Details concerning the number of casualties and the amount of damage inflicted are not yet available, but unofficial initial reports are that both were considerable. Further details will be announced over this station as soon as additional reports are received.*

All three Japanese boys had stopped eating to listen to the broadcast. As the music resumed and an excited chattering in both English and Japanese started up all around them, thin Tommy Masamura said, "The sons of bitches!"

Plump Joe Harukawa emitted a nervous little chuckle. "Well, that takes care of our worries about what the hell we're going to do when we get out of high school. We're going to be in the Army."

"The Marines for me," Jimmy Katsu said, flexing the muscles of his thick arms. "You sisters can wait to be drafted into the Army."

"Fuck you, buddy," Tommy told him amiably. "What makes you think you could make it through boot camp?"

"Just watch me," Jimmy said with confidence.

"Maybe we could all join the Marines together," the plump boy said hopefully. "Get in the same outfit."

"Sure," Jimmy said with enthusiasm. "What say, Tommy?"

Tommy shrugged his lean shoulders. "Guess I ought to go along to keep you guys from stumbling over your own feet."

They were all too excited to finish eating. Dumping the

remnants of their food into a trash can, by tacit agreement they headed for the nearest bus stop where a Boyle Heights bus stopped. Their initial plan to pick up girls forgotten, it now seemed urgent to all of them to get home and sit by the radio.

When a Boyle Heights bus came along and its door opened, they could hear an excited buzz of conversation among the half dozen passengers already on the bus. Presumably they had just received word of the Japanese attack, too, and the momentous news had broken down the normal reserve between strangers on the same bus.

Conversation died abruptly as the three Japanese teen-agers got on the bus. The driver watched silently and unsmilingly as they dropped their fares. The bus started to move as they walked toward the seat at the rear, where they could all sit together, and the other passengers stared at them as they went by.

One overweight woman was glaring at them with open hostility. The squat Jimmy, bringing up the rear, paused to glare back and say with teen-age cockiness, "We didn't do it, lady. We're natural-born Americans."

She sucked in an indignant breath. A burly man of about thirty seated behind her said, "Don't get smart, Jap."

Flexing his muscles, Jimmy let his eyes glitter at the man. For several seconds the burly man met his gaze, but then his eyes shifted away. Jimmy moved on to take his seat with the others.

"Sure gave us the treatment, didn't they," Joe said with an uneasy laugh. "You'd think we personally dropped the goddamned bombs."

"Screw 'em," Jimmy said. "Assholes like that don't bother me."

Tommy said, "You're lucky that asshole with the big shoulders that you stared down didn't know you're muscle-bound."

"Screw you too, pal," Jimmy told him.

When they got off the bus, they decided to go to Tommy Masamura's house. They usually gathered there instead of at either of the other boys' homes, because the Masamuras were the most Americanized of the three families. All three families had immigrated to America more than twenty years before, but the Harukawas and the Katsus still clung to many of the traditional ways. In both families only Japanese was spoken in the home unless there were American visitors, although all four parents spoke English with hardly any accent. The shoes of all visitors had to be left on the porch before entering. But most embarrassing to both boys was their mother's insistence on the traditional Japanese subservience of women to their male superiors. Both boys hated it when they brought home school friends, particularly non-Japanese friends, and their mothers greeted them with submissive bows.

At the Masamura home, on the other hand, the only sign of Japanese culture was a few Japanese drawings on the walls and a few Japanese vases. English was the language spoken, and customs were strictly American. This was largely because Tommy's father, whose original name was Makoto Masamura, but who had long since shortened it to Matt, was a loan officer in a downtown bank, and through his job had developed many more American friends than he had Japanese friends. Joe's father worked for a Japanese importer, and Jimmy's was a baker in a bakery employing Japanese help almost exclusively. Neither of these families had ever developed any close American friends.

Tommy's mother and father were seated in the front room, listening to the radio, when the three boys came in. Matt Masamura raised his hand in greeting, then motioned for silence. The boys halted just inside the door and stood listening to the bulletin coming over the air.

The announcer was saying:

> *No figures are as yet available on actual casualties or damage from the Japanese attack on Pearl Harbor, but it is now officially admitted that both were extremely high. It is now reported that virtually the entire Pacific fleet of the United States Navy was anchored in the harbor when the bombers struck.*

There is an unconfirmed report that several battleships were sunk in the harbor, and that many other ships were heavily damaged.

Stay tuned to this station for up-to-the-minute developments on the story of this dastardly sneak attack, and the reactions it has brought from around the world.

Music began to come from the radio. The three boys went over to seat themselves in a row on the sofa.

Tommy said to his father, "We heard it on the radio over in the Japanese section."

Mrs. Masamura said, "It's terrible. I'm so ashamed that Japanese people could be so treacherous."

In a reflective tone Mr. Masamura said, "It means war, of course."

"Means?" Tommy said with raised eyebrows. "It *is* war, isn't it?"

"Not officially, just yet," his father said. "Just before you came in, the announcer said President Roosevelt is calling a joint session of Congress tomorrow morning. No doubt he will ask for a declaration of war, and get one." After a long pause, he added, "I'm afraid we are in for a hard time."

Jimmy said, "You mean because we're Japanese, sir?"

Mr. Masamura nodded. "In wartime people tend to lose their perspectives, Jimmy."

"Yeah, there was an old bag on the bus." After thinking, Jimmy added, "Fact is, everybody on the bus, including the driver, kind of lost their perspectives. And maybe some of 'em weren't even born here, like me and Joe and Tommy."

"We may all have to adjust ourselves to a certain amount of harassment from unthinking people," Mr. Masamura said.

During the afternoon repeated bulletins came over the air. Eventually it was reported that the attack had been by 360 Japanese planes, and that the United States had lost the battleships *Arizona, California, Oklahoma* and *West Virginia*, plus the mine-layer *Oglala* and the target ship *Utah*. In addition 174 American planes on the ground at nearby Hickam Field had been destroyed.

At 7:00 P.M. the news came over the air that Japan had declared war on the United States an hour earlier, thus beating the United States to the punch on that too.

The next morning President Franklin Roosevelt, speaking before the joint session of Congress, called December 7 "a date which will live in infamy," and asked for a declaration of war. Congress obliged.

The harassment Tommy Masamura's father prophesied began almost immediately. At high school the three boys' non-Japanese friends studiously ignored them. They were met by hostile glares from strangers everywhere they went.

Just before Christmas Matt Masamura was transferred from his loan office position to the bookkeeping department, where he would be out of public view. It was a considerable demotion in responsibility, but the bank was decent enough to keep him at the same salary.

Jimmy Katsu's father was unaffected, because his baking job kept him out of public view anyway, and most of his co-workers were Japanese. But war with Japan cut off the stock-in-trade of the importer employing Joe Harukawa's father. He was laid off.

The parents of the three boys tended to accept their harsh treatment by the American public with stoicism, but the boys' reaction was to fight back. They got in the habit of being together always, and they belligerently returned hostile gazes with challenging glares.

They had one fight at school, but only one. A group of six boys began taunting them one day, and they took all six to the cleaners. Actually Joe and Tommy whipped only one each, and Jimmy handled the other four, but it was the group that gained the reputation of being a risky bunch to tangle with. Their schoolmates left them alone after that.

Despite all the harassment, in the beginning the three boys still planned to join the Marines as soon as they graduated from high school. But then not just the unthinking public but the highest officials in the land, up to and including the President, began to turn against them.

As public fear mounted that Japanese-Americans would feel their primary allegiance lay with Japan, and thus constituted a "fifth-column" threat, Congress reacted to the growing public pressure by debating the possible "relocation" of all Japanese on the West Coast.

The parents of all three boys even accepted that threat with stoicism. But the effect on the boys themselves was drastic. They were outraged that their own country, in which they were natural-born citizens, should brand them as potential traitors without trial, and without even an investigation of any sort.

All thought of joining the Marine Corps evaporated in bitterness. When, early in 1942, the relocation program was actually put into effect, the six parents, Joe Harukawa's older sister, and Jimmy Katsu's twelve-year-old brother all meekly marched off to the train station. But all three boys defiantly refused to go to what they referred to as a "concentration camp." They had to be forcibly hauled off in handcuffs, snarling at their guards and calling them Nazi storm troopers.

When Marion Hedgepeth saw them defiantly standing with their backs to the flag during the Retreat ceremony, they had been in the camp near Bidwell more than a year and a half, and had celebrated two birthdays there. At nineteen they were no less bitter at their treatment by the United States government than they had been when forcibly dragged from their homes.

They were the Peck's bad boys of the camp, almost constantly in trouble and constantly giving trouble.

Chapter 13

Marion got back to the Oasis Café at five minutes of six. A dark-haired, slightly plump girl of about twenty was just coming from behind the counter carrying a dinner plate in her right hand, and with three more stacked along her left arm. She took them over to a booth where two couples sat together.

This being the middle of the dinner hour, most of the booths were filled, and several people sat at the two counters. Marion looked around, but failed to spot Rose.

He took a stool next to the wall at the counter facing the kitchen. Conscious that everyone at the counter was looking at him, he summoned a shy smile for all of them and was rewarded with a series of answering smiles.

The dark-haired girl bustled behind the counter, approached him with a wide grin and said, "Hi. You must be Hedge."

"Yes," he admitted, grinning back.

"I'm Thelma. You want anything, or just waiting for Rose?"

"Just waiting."

"She'll be right out," Thelma said. She went to lift another order from the service counter and deliver it to a counter customer.

Rose came from the kitchen carrying a purse in one hand and Marion's little canvas bag in the other. He got to his feet and went over to meet her as she came through the opening in the counter next to the register.

"Hi," she said.

"Hi," he echoed, gazing at her in a way that made her blush.

He took his bag from her and stepped aside to let her precede him to the door. But she paused to look back at Thelma, now filling coffee cups at the counter.

"Just a minute, I want you to meet Thelma," Rose said.

"We already met," Marion said.

Overhearing, Thelma called, "Yeah, I introduced myself, Rose."

"Oh," Rose said. "Okay, see you Monday, Thelma."

"Have fun," Thelma said. "Bye, Hedge."

He threw her a smile. "Nice to have met you."

He followed after Rose, hurried to reach past her and open the door, and closed it behind them. When they had crossed the graveled parking lot to the sidewalk, she turned right. He fell in on her left, next to the curb, and shifted his bag to his left hand. She shifted her purse to her right.

"It's not far," she said. "Only two blocks."

"I wouldn't care if it was two miles," he said gallantly.

She smiled at him.

"You told Thelma you'd see her Monday," he said. "You don't work weekends?"

"No, I'm off."

"Two whole days," he said, pleased.

Then he wondered why he was sounding so pleased, since he would have to move on in the morning. Or would he, necessarily? Inasmuch as he was only going home to disgrace, what difference would a couple more days make? He decided to see what developed before he thought about it any more.

A block beyond the Oasis Café they turned right on one of the gravel roads.

"We don't have street signs in this town," Rose said. "But if you're interested, this is Finley Way."

Glancing at the old-fashioned houses lining both sides of the street, he asked, "This the street you live on?"

"Around the corner, on Buttercup Lane."

"Now there's a nice name for a street," he said. "Don't think I ever heard that name for one before."

"Story is they had to dig up a field of buttercups when they put it in about a hundred years ago."

As they came to the corner and turned right, the backs of her left hand and his right accidentally brushed together. Both jerked them away as though they had received electric shocks, then they stopped to look at each other, and both suddenly laughed. She held out her left hand, he engulfed it in his oversized right, and they continued on hand in hand.

The Hudkins' house was the third from the corner, a big, late-Victorian frame house of two stories with a wide front porch containing a porch swing. Like most houses in the town, it was painted white with green trim.

Not knowing how her parents would react to seeing a strange boy holding their daughter's hand, Marion tried to drop it as they turned in at the walk. But she only tightened her own grip, led him up the porch steps and into the house.

As the screen door banged shut behind them, three people appeared from three different directions. They had entered a wide hallway, with a staircase to the second floor straight ahead, and with open sliding doors on either side. The banging screen door was a signal for Rose's father to appear from the parlor on the right, her mother to come from the kitchen through the dining room on the left, and for her thirteen-year-old brother to come racing down the stairs.

Mr. Hudkins was a tall, distinguished-looking man of forty with graying temples and gold-rimmed spectacles. He was dressed in a gray pin-striped suit and a silver necktie. Mrs. Hudkins, a couple of years younger than her husband, was a slim, attractive, clear-skinned woman in a blue party dress with an apron over it. She looked so much like Rose that a dictum of his own mother's popped into his mind: "If you want to know what a girl will look like when she begins to age, look at her mother."

Barney Hudkins was a skinny, coltish youngster whose red nose indicated he had a bad head cold. He had on a blue serge suit and a red necktie and looked as though both made him uncomfortable.

Marion dropped Rose's hand, this time successfully, swept off his cap and tucked it into his belt.

Rose said, "Dad, Mom, this is Hedge—Marion Hedgepeth."

Her mother said, "We're glad you could come, Hedge," quite obviously meaning it. Holding out his hand, Rose's father said, "Welcome to our home, Hedge."

Clasping the hand, Marion managed to get out a shy, "Appreciate the invitation, sir." Then, turning toward Mrs. Hudkins, he said, "Pleased to meet you, ma'am."

Rose indicated her younger brother, who had halted at the bottom of the stairs to gawk at Marion. "This is Barney, Hedge."

Marion walked over with his hand outstretched. "Hi, Barney."

Both astonished and delighted at being afforded such adult treatment, Barney clasped the hand and shook it heartily. "Hi, Hedge," he said, quite suddenly falling into a state of hero worship.

Mrs. Hudkins said crisply, "Rose, I imagine you'll want to freshen up before dinner. Barney, while your sister's getting ready, show Hedge where he's going to sleep, then show him where to wash up, if he wants."

"Yes, ma'am," Barney said. "Come on, Hedge."

Barney started up the stairs. Marion let Rose precede him before following. At the top of the stairs Rose turned left, and Barney led Marion the other way.

The room they entered was that of a typical high school frosh. Two pennants hung on the wall, one lettered RIVERTON HIGH SCHOOL, the other lettered CHICAGO CUBS. In front of the window there was a desk piled with school books, and a small bookcase with several model airplanes sitting on it. Against a side wall was a solid-looking double-decker bunk.

"You can have the lower," Barney said generously.

As Marion set his bag and cap on the lower bunk, Barney took out a handkerchief and blew his nose.

"Bad cold?" Marion asked with sympathy.

"Yeah," the boy said. "Hope I don't give it to you."

"You don't catch cold unless you're a little run down," Marion said. "I'm in pretty good shape."

"Yeah, you sure are that," Barney said admiringly. "Come on and I'll show you the bathroom."

Barney left him alone in the bathroom and went back downstairs. Marion washed his hands and face, examined his reflection in the mirror and decided he still came up to Marine standards of neatness, thanks to the farmer's wife where he had stayed the previous night.

When he got back downstairs, he found Mr. Hudkins and Barney together in the front room. Rose's father sat in an easy chair to one side of a large fireplace, Barney sat in the center of an old-fashioned mohair sofa. As Marion entered, Mr. Hudkins folded the paper he was reading and laid it on an end table.

Marion said, "Don't let me interrupt your reading, sir."

Smiling, Mr. Hudkins said, "I had finished. Sit down, Hedge."

Marion chose an overstuffed chair. He sat erect, hands folded in his lap, slightly ill-at-ease.

Mr. Hudkins said, "So you're from Missouri."

Startled, Marion said, "Yes, sir. How did you know?"

"No great mystery. Rose told her mother when she phoned she was bringing you home, and her mother told me. Where in Missouri?"

"Crystal City, sir. Just a little place, around three thousand."

Barney said, "Compared to Bidwell, that's a metropolis."

Rose came into the room. She had changed into a pink-and-white print dress and had tied her chestnut hair into a ponytail with a pink ribbon. Marion popped to his feet and tried to keep an adoring expression from showing on his face.

"Keep your seat, Hedge," she said. "I can't stay, because I have to go help Mom."

Mr. Hudkins said, "Ran into Sheriff Wenzel this afternoon, Hedge. He told me he gave you a ride into town."

Still standing, Marion wrenched his gaze from Rose to look at her father. "Yes, sir."

"Understand you don't have any family."

Wishing he had never told that lie, Marion said, "Well, aunts and uncles. I have a place to stay at home."

Rose said, "I'll call you when dinner's ready," and went out of the room.

Ten minutes later she returned to call them to dinner. When they crossed the hall into the dining room, Marion stared at the table in astonishment. It was a large table, big enough to seat eight, and it was absolutely jammed with food. There was a pot roast, a bowl of mashed potatoes, gravy, several vegetables, hot rolls, and even a pie and a chocolate cake.

Mr. Hudkins seated himself at the head of the table. Marion was given the place of honor to his right, and Barney sat to his left. Rose sat next to Marion and Mrs. Hudkins next to Barney.

After saying grace, Mr. Hudkins began to carve the roast. When the plates were all served and distributed, the other dishes were passed around so that all could take what they pleased.

Amid the aura of pleasant family relationship and the feeling that he was genuinely welcome in their home, Marion began to relax. It was a fine family, Marion thought, about the finest he had ever met, other than his own parents.

As he helped himself to mashed potatoes, he said, "I like eating this way. I mean, everything on the table at the same time."

"It's the way we do here," Rose said.

Mr. Hudkins said with a twinkle in his eye, "I imagine it's the nature of rich people to hide dessert."

Everyone laughed. These were certainly fine people, Marion thought. He was feeling more and more at home by the minute.

Chapter 14

Marion passed the mashed potatoes to Rose and accepted the gravy bowl from Mr. Hudkins.

"How do they eat in the Marines?" young Barney asked.

Because his total Marine experience had been at boot camp, Marion automatically answered in terms of that experience. As he ladled gravy onto his potatoes, he said, "Well, Barney, in boot camp in Dago—that's what we call San Diego—you can get as much as you want. But you have to finish. Every last bite. And why? Because when you carry your tray out there's an inspector, and you have to show him. One time I had this gob of butter, and he said, 'Eat it,' and I said I was full, and he said, 'Eat it,' and I asked if I could go back and get some bread, and he said, 'Eat it,' and so I had to eat that big gob of butter all by itself. Just try that sometime."

"What if you said you wouldn't eat it?" Barney asked, fascinated.

Shuddering slightly, Marion said, "Don't want to think about that."

He passed the gravy to Rose and took a bowl of peas from Mr. Hudkins. The latter said, "Then the food overseas must be some shock."

"Yes, sir," Marion said.

'What do you eat overseas?" Barney asked.

Marion was about to say, "C rations," figuring that would be a safe answer, when Mr. Hudkins beat him to it by saying, "Spam, Barney. Chicken-fried Spam, Spam and raisins, Spam and eggs, powdered, of course." He paused at Marion's surprised look and smiled. "One of our teachers has a boy in England. B-seventeens."

Marion wasn't at all sure that the food in the Pacific would be the same as in England, but he was willing to accept it. He said, "That's right, Barney. Spam."

The serving bowls all eventually made the circuit of the table, and everyone began to eat. For some moments there was no conversation.

Then Rose suddenly asked, "You like football, Hedge?"

Surprised by the question, he glanced at her and said, "Why sure, Rose."

Barney said, "Bet you played in high school."

"Yeah," Marion admitted.

"First string?"

"Uh-huh," Marion said, slightly embarrassed, and wondering why, because here was something that wasn't a lie, like his Marine background.

"Backfield?"

"End," Marion said. For some reason he didn't want to mention that he had been an all-conference end, possibly because down-playing his football accomplishments in some way helped compensate for the lie he was living now. He said with self-depreciation, "Small place like Crystal City, doesn't take much to make varsity."

Rose said, "I'm off tomorrow and Sunday, you know. Season's first game is at Riverton tomorrow. We usually go."

Marion was conscious of all eyes being on him, waiting for his response. He wanted to stay. He wanted to stay forever, but by now his parents might have been notified of his unfit discharge and would be worried sick about where he was.

Sensing his distress, Mr. Hudkins said in a gentle tone, "We won't urge you if you're anxious to get home, but you're welcome to stay as long as you like."

Marion came to a decision. "Then thanks. No hurry to be anywhere."

Everyone at the table smiled. Rose said, "Then you'll go to the game?"

"Sure, I'd like that."

Barney said matter-of-factly, "We're going to get slaughtered."

"Oh?" Rose said with mild indignation. "We would've won last year if—" Unable to think of just what contingency would have let Riverton win, she let it trail off.

Barney said, "If the other team didn't show up."

Everyone at the table laughed, including Barney.

When plates were finally empty, Mrs. Hudkins said to Marion, "More, Hedge?"

He hesitated, glanced at all the food still in serving bowls, plus the two-thirds still remaining of the huge roast, and gave in. "Well, it's so good," he said, passing his plate to Mr. Hudkins.

As Mr. Hudkins carved more meat, Barney's gaze fixed on Marion in open hero worship. Despite his guilt, Marion couldn't resist playing up to the boy. But again the trouble was that all he really knew about the Marines was boot camp.

He said, "Know something, Barney? In boot camp, if they catch you singing, they put a bucket on your head and *make* you sing."

Rose said, "Why, that's not nice."

"But it does cut down on the noise, I imagine," Mr. Hudkins said, twinkling again.

"Yes, sir. And hands in your pockets? They fill 'em up with sand and sew 'em shut."

Mr. Hudkins handed back his plate. Marion began to take small portions of potatoes and vegetables.

"But it's better than being overseas, I bet," Barney said.

Misinterpreting Marion's suddenly stricken face, Mrs. Hudkins said quietly to Barney, "I'm sure he'd rather not talk about it, dear."

Marion felt gratitude. He *couldn't* talk about it.

In a reflective voice Mr. Hudkins said, "Unfortunately, there's not much to talk about except the war. Oh, we're going to win, but what I find myself thinking about is afterwards. What all you boys will be like."

Puzzled, Marion glanced up. "Beg pardon?"

Rose looked at her father in alarm, thinking he was going to start advertising the virtues of living in Bidwell, trying to sell the place, and in the process convincing

Hedge that he was being considered as a potential son-in-law.

"I can't really say what worries me," her father continued. "It's just a feeling that nothing's going to be the same. The old ways gone. That B-seventeen boy I was telling you about, for instance. Writes he'd like to live in London after the war."

Rose's alarm evaporated.

Marion said, "Well, London might be all right, but you can keep San Diego. Nice weather, but too many sailors."

Rose said, "Oh, Dad, Ray Burden's just talking. He'll kiss the ground when he gets back."

Pursing his lips, her father gave a nod admitting that possibility. "Some things may be better," he said reflectively, then added after a pause, "They'll have to be. But I still think about the old ways."

After dinner Rose and Mrs. Hudkins did the dishes, while Mr. Hudkins, Marion and Barney retired to the front room. Marion offered to dry the dishes, but neither Rose nor her mother would hear of it.

Mr. Hudkins settled in his chair, Marion took the same chair he had before dinner, and Barney resumed his place on the sofa. Mr. Hudkins loaded and lit a pipe.

"You smoke, Hedge?" he asked.

"No, sir."

Mr. Hudkins nodded approvingly. "Be wise if you never start." He fixed his gaze on Barney. "I've heard of youngsters as young as thirteen getting caught smoking in the garage. Very hard on the seat of the pants."

Flushing, Barney blew his nose, then pulled at his tight shirt collar. "Can I take this stuff off now, Dad?"

Considering, his father finally nodded. "No reason to wear a coat and tie all evening. But hang them up. And don't change into those awful Levis. Keep on the trousers and shirt you're wearing."

"Yes, sir," Barney said, bouncing to his feet and running from the room.

"Think I'll get a little more comfortable myself," Mr.

Scenes on the following pages are from the Columbia Pictures presentation, BABY BLUE MARINE.

Jan-Michael Vincent as WWII Marine Corps recruit, Marion Hedgepeth.

Glynnis O'Connor as Rose Hudkins, a young waitress Marion meets in a small western town.

At San Diego Marine Corps Base, Marion gets fouled up doing the manual-of-arms.

In a servicemen's bar, Marion meets a Marine Raider, a hardened combat veteran.

Later, he awakens to find himself drunk and stripped in an alley.

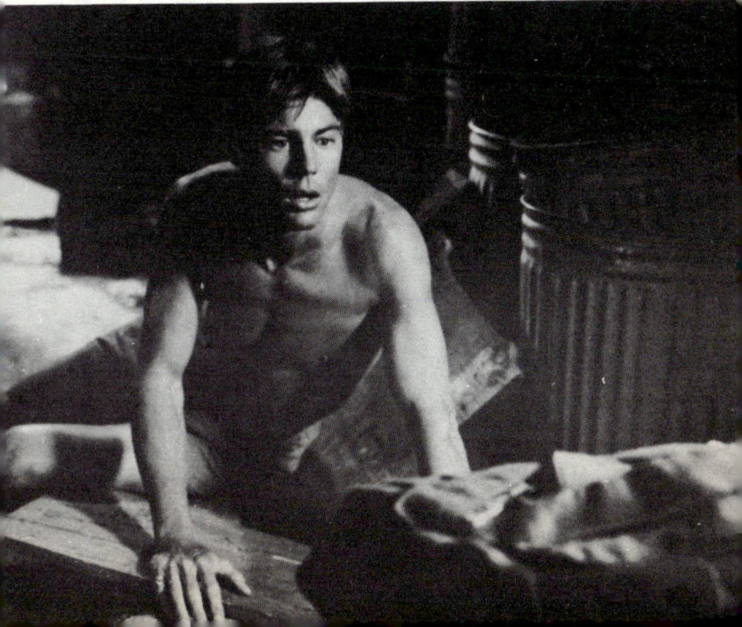

Marion travels homeward, now wearing the Raider's uniform. In the Oasis Café where she works, Rose is instantly attracted to Marion.

At a nearby Japanese relocation camp, Marion salutes the flag during Retreat.

Rose's family have Marion as honored guest for dinner.

Marion stays overnight at Rose's house.

Rose is proud to be seen with Marion as she takes him around town.

At the local theater, the young couple are touched by the movie they've seen.

The next day, Marion and Rose surrender to their love.

When three Japanese youths escape from the camp, Marion is forced to take part in a crucial, tragic situation.

Hudkins said, rising to his feet and slipping out of his suit coat. "Like to hang up your jacket too, Hedge?"

"Don't mind if I do, sir," Marion said, getting up also.

Mr. Hudkins led the way into the hall, hung his coat in the hall closet, and handed a hanger to Marion. When they returned to the front room, Marion decided to loosen his tie and collar. He relaxed in his chair, feeling very much at home.

Barney returned, coatless and tieless, and with his white shirt open at the throat. A few minutes later Rose and Mrs. Hudkins came in. Marion immediately rose to his feet.

"Like to play some Monopoly, Hedge?" Rose asked.

"Sure," he said.

"Me too?" Barney inquired.

"Why not?" Marion said.

Barney gave him a delighted grin.

While Rose went after the Monopoly set, Mrs. Hudkins lifted a ball of knitting with two needles stuck in it and a half-completed sweater from atop the Chickering spinet in a corner of the parlor and seated herself in a chair on the opposite side of the fireplace from her husband. When Rose returned, she set the Monopoly board on the floor near the door, which put it clear across the long room from her parents. Mr. Hudkins rose long enough to switch on an Atwater Kent console radio, then returned to his chair and contentedly puffed his pipe.

Music came from the radio. Rose, Marion and Barney rolled the dice for high, and Rose won first turn.

The game had been going on for about fifteen minutes, Mrs. Hudkins was still knitting, and Mr. Hudkins was still smoking his pipe when commentator Edward R. Murrow came on the air.

In his sonorous voice the famed commentator said:

> *This is London. Early this morning we heard the bombers going out. It was the sound of a giant factory in the sky. It seemed to shake the old gray stone buildings in this bruised and battered city beside the*

Thames. The sound was heavier, more triumphant than ever before.

Marion paused in the act of casting the dice to listen to the voice on the radio for a moment, then went ahead and threw them. Rose and Barney were paying no attention to the broadcast, their full attention being centered on Marion. Barney's expression was one of hero worship, Rose's that of a girl in love.

Murrow was saying:

Earlier I had attended the briefing. The atmosphere was that of a school or a church. The weatherman gave us the weather. The pilots were reminded that Berlin is Germany's greatest center of war production. The intelligence officer told us how many heavy and light ack-ack guns, how many searchlights—

Leaning toward her husband, Mrs. Hudkins whispered, "Tom. Oh, Tom."

Mr. Hudkins pulled his attention from the radio long enough to glance at her. She nodded toward the Monopoly players. Glancing that way, he immediately saw what his wife wanted him to notice. It was the expression on his daughter's face.

The expression saddened him. Not because she had so suddenly fallen in love, nor because he had any objection to the boy she had chosen to love. It was only because it could last no more than a day or two. Then the boy would move on, and he had no faith in the axiom that absence made the heart grow fonder. The chance of the romance lasting the duration of the war, which promised to go on for some years yet, seemed to him remote.

As he watched, Hedge rolled the dice, moved his racing car marker and pretended dismay at the result. Delighted, Rose held out her hand for payment. Mr. Hudkins wrenched his attention back to the radio report.

Murrow was saying:

> *The big Canadian with the slow, easy grin had printed "Berlin" at the top of his pad, and embellished it with a scroll. The redheaded English boy with the two-weeks' old moustache was the last to leave the room.*

Across the room Barney crowed, "You're on my hotel, Rose. Pay me."

Chapter 15

Later they had music. Mrs. Hudkins played the spinet, Mr. Hudkins accompanied her on the mandolin, and Rose played the accordion. Barney turned the music sheets for his mother.

The musicians were not enormously talented, but they at least partly made up for that with their enthusiasm. It was so apparent that they were going all-out to entertain the combat veteran who had accidentally come to them that Marion was more touched than ashamed. They played all the old favorites, such as "Drink to Me Only with Thine Eyes," "The Touch of Sylvia's Hand" and "Wabash Moon," plus some classic popular music such as "Stardust." Despite an occasional false note, Marion thought it was the most beautiful music he had ever heard.

Eventually, just as the trio ended a piece more or less together, Mrs. Hudkins glanced over at the clock on the fireplace mantel. "Nine o'clock," she said. "Anyone like coffee or cocoa?"

"I could use some coffee," Mr. Hudkins said, setting his mandolin in a corner.

Rose started putting her accordion back into its case. "Cocoa for me. And I think I'll make some fudge."

"I'll have coffee," Marion said.

"Me, too," Barney said hopefully.

His mother said, "You'll have cocoa, young man."

Barney shrugged resignedly. He hadn't really expected to get his preference anyway.

They all repaired to the kitchen. It was a large, old-fashioned kitchen, but there was a modern gas stove and an electric refrigerator. Centered in the room was a big round table with a red-and-white checkered oilcloth cover. Mr. Hudkins, Marion and Barney sat at the table while Rose began to make fudge and Mrs. Hudkins started the coffee perculator and began to heat milk for cocoa.

Barney said, "Can you tell us anything at all about overseas, Hedge?"

His mother and father and Rose all gave him admonishing looks. He looked so abashed, Marion felt sorry for him.

"It's all right," he said. "There's some things nobody minds talking about. It isn't all shooting."

Barney's face brightened.

Having committed himself, Marion searched desperately for something to tell. Suddenly he recalled an overheard conversation between two D.I.s, both combat veterans, at boot camp. The recollection solved his problem.

"You know what C rations are, Barney?"

"Sure, Danny Phelps let me taste one. Kind of hard, bitter chocolate bars." Barney made a face. "I didn't like it."

"That's D rations," Marion said. He was on safe ground here, because as part of boot training recruits were introduced to all three standard emergency rations: C, D and K. "You carry them on patrol out in the jungle as emergency rations, for when you can't light a fire. C rations comes in cans. There's beans and hash and stew, and what they do is the cooks boil a big pot of water full of C ration cans, and when you go through the chow line, you fish one out of the pot. When you open the can, you've got a hot meal. It's not too bad, whether you get beans, hash or stew. The hash isn't even bad cold, which is how you get it sometimes when you're on the march and there's not enough time for the cooks to heat water. But—"

When he let it hang in order to build suspense, Barney said. "But what?"

"But the one can is only part of it. C rations comes in a set of two cans. The second one feels light, because what it has in it is some kind of cracker-like biscuits, some hard candy, sugar, and the makings for your beverage. Some have powdered instant coffee, others have lemonade powder."

"Where would you get the ice for the lemonade?" Barney asked.

"You wouldn't. But that's not the worst part. Those cans aren't marked to tell you whether there's powdered coffee or lemon powder inside. It's sure some thrill to pull into position about two in the morning in a pouring rain, have the cooks start coffee water boiling, be all set for a nice hot cup of coffee with your C rations, open that second can and find out you're going to have lukewarm lemonade."

Everyone laughed. Mr. Hudkins said, "Something ought to be done about that."

Still quoting the overheard conversation between the two D.I.s, Marion said, "Oh, there will be. An I.G. visited our outfit once just in time for a C ration meal, and drew the lemon powder. An I.G.'s a member of the Inspector General's office. They go around listening to complaints by guys in the field. He said he was going to report it to Washington. So probably about the time the war ends, they'll start labeling those cans."

Everyone laughed again. Then Mrs. Hudkins checked the heating milk, decided it was hot enough, and made cocoa for Barney, Rose and herself. Placing empty cups before her husband and Marion, she said, "Coffee in about five minutes. How's the fudge coming, Rose?"

Giving it a stir, Rose said, "Ready to pour."

She poured it into a pan, then set the pan in the refrigerator for quick cooling.

Barney said, "Tell us something about your buddies, Hedge."

Which ones, Marion wondered wryly? Pop Mosley, Rupe Huffman and B. J. Dobbs? Then he thought of Andy. With one part of his mind he rejected any further fantasizing as a shameless trick on such fine people. But another part urged him to repay them for the wonderful time they were showing him. And the repayment they wanted was exactly what he was giving them.

He gave in to the second part.

"There was a fellow I really liked," he said. "Not in my outfit. Met him—met him in the jungle on patrol once. We hit it off real good. Andy his name was. Forget his last name."

The perking coffee pot suddenly stopped gurgling. "Coffee's ready," Mrs. Hudkins announced.

She unplugged the pot, brought it to the table and filled Marion's and her husband's cups. Setting it down on the table, she seated herself next to Barney. Rose opened the refrigerator door to test the fudge with a tentative finger, then closed it again.

"What about this fellow?" Barney asked. "Was he a Marine too?"

Marion nodded. "Funny guy, Andy. Talked so quiet, but was he tough!"

"Tougher'n you?" Barney inquired with obvious disbelief that such was possible.

Giving him a quizzical look, Marion considered the question for a time before saying, "Never wanted to tangle with him."

Rose said in a mildly scolding voice, "Barney, Marines have enough without fighting each other."

"That's it, Rose," Marion said with approval. "No, Andy was a funny one. Snow-white hair."

"White?" Mrs. Hudkins said.

"Yes, ma'am, and not even old enough to vote."

Mr. Hudkins said judiciously, "That can happen to hair. Shock. Had he seen a lot of action?"

"He'd never say," Marion said truthfully. "But he sure didn't look just twenty."

There was general silence as they all reflected on the terrible things war could do to young men. Rose opened the refrigerator again, tested the fudge, and this time lifted out the pan. Setting it on the table, she began cutting it into squares.

In a transparent, but nevertheless successful effort to lighten the mood, she said, "You think Marine fudge ought to have whiskey in it?"

Reaching for a piece, Marion sampled it and said, "Ummm. No."

It was a verdict. She smiled her pleasure that the fudge had turned out well.

Seating herself next to Marion, she said, "Didn't have any idea you'd come here, did you?"

He looked at her, his heart almost breaking with love for her, and with despair at the hopelessness of the situation. "Just a week ago," he said in such a low voice that she had to strain to hear him. "I—well, I sure was different."

Blushing, but not quite sure what she was blushing about, Rose covered her confusion by pushing the fudge pan across the table to Barney and her father. Both took pieces and pushed it on to Mrs. Hudkins.

When Mrs. Hudkins had taken a piece, she said lightly to Rose, "Aren't you going to eat any of your own fudge?"

"I know what's in it," Rose said, then giggled and took a piece.

At ten o'clock Mr. Hudkins suggested that since they were going to have a big day tomorrow, they had better get some sleep. Rose immediately got up and began carrying cups to the sink to wash.

Mrs. Hudkins said, "Hedge, if you have any laundry to be done, just drop it down the clothes chute in the bathroom in the morning. I don't suppose you have much, though, just carrying that little bag."

"One change," he said. "I been washing things out in Red Cross Service Clubs." Then, deciding his traveling so light required some explanation, he said, "Shipped my other stuff home by Greyhound."

Marion offered to dry the cups for Rose, and this time there was no objection either from her or Mrs. Hudkins. It was hardly a big chore, and it gave them a few moments to be alone.

"We'll go on up," Mrs. Hudkins said, rising to her feet. "See you in the morning, Hedge."

"Yes, ma'am. Thanks for everything. Supper was wonderful, and the whole evening too."

"You're more than welcome," she said.

Marion went over to the sink, picked up a dish towel

and waited for Rose to wash and rinse cups. Mr. Hudkins got up from the table, told Marion and Rose good-night, and left the room.

Mrs. Hudkins said to her still seated son, "Come on, Barney."

"I'll wait for Hedge," the boy said.

"You'll come right now and get into bed, young man," his mother informed him. "Hedge can find his way to your room without you."

Reluctantly he got up and followed his mother from the room. As he went out the door, he said over his shoulder to Marion, "See you upstairs."

When Rose and Marion climbed the stairs a few minutes later, they paused in the upper hallway to look at each other.

"The whole evening's sure been swell," he said.

"I liked it too, Hedge."

They continued to look at each other. "Good night," she said.

"Good night," he said without moving.

They looked at each other some more, with fixed smiles on their faces, until she finally said, "Oh, Hedge!" moved in close and stood on tiptoe in order to give him a quick kiss on the mouth. Then she was running down the hallway to her own room.

Marion looked after her until she disappeared. Then he turned the other way toward Barney's room.

The light was on in the boy's room, and Barney was in bed in the top bunk. He smiled at Marion and Marion smiled back. Marion got his toilet kit from the canvas bag, went up the hall to the bathroom and brushed his teeth. When he came back, he stripped to his underwear, carefully hung his uniform on a hanger in Barney's closet, turned off the light and climbed into bed, He lay on his back, hands behind his head, thinking about the wonderful evening.

"Night, Hedge," Barney said.

"Night, Barney."

There was a period of silence, then a sniffle from above, and, "Hedge?"

"Yeah?"

"Could I ask a favor?"

"Name it, Barney."

There was another silence before the boy said, "Well, it's about Barney. Rather be called Ace."

Marion smiled into the darkness. "Ace Hudkins. Good middleweight."

"How'd you know?" Barney asked in a delighted tone.

"Read."

This time there was a longer silence before Barney said tentatively, "Hedge?"

"Yeah, Ace?"

"Think it'll still be on when I grow up."

God, he wanted to go to war, Marion thought. Maybe go to Marine boot camp, get busted out and come home in disgrace. Or make it and end up a dead hero. He said, "Hope not."

"What's it like out there?"

Marion thought back to the Los Angeles tavern where he had asked Andy much the same question, and had listened so avidly to his reply. "Oh, weather's nice and warm. A little rain every day. And the sun goes down fast."

"I mean the other thing. The way it is."

Marion was silent.

After waiting a while, Barney said, "Not like the movies, huh?"

"Not really," Marion said.

"Lots of noise and smoke?"

All he knew about it was ten minutes' conversation with Andy, Marion thought. He said, "There's that."

Nothing more came from above for a long time. Marion had decided the boy must have gone to sleep when he asked in a barely audible whisper, "You ever have to kill anybody?"

Marion thought about that for some time, and finally gave Andy's answer. "Everybody did."

Barney emitted a sigh. "Ever think about it?"

"Try not to."

A sniffle came from above, then the sound of the boy

blowing his nose. Apparently he had a handkerchief under his pillow. "I'm sorry, Hedge."

"Okay to ask," Marion said.

"I mean you having to think about it."

God, if only he were a real Marine back from overseas, Marion thought. He said heavily, "Thanks, Ace."

"Good night, Hedge."

"Night, Ace."

This time there was no more conversation.

Chapter 16

In the morning Barney was still sleeping when Marion got up. Stripping off his underwear and putting on his trousers in case he ran into anyone in the hallway, he carried his bag to the bathroom in one hand and his dirty laundry in the other. As he passed the stairway, he heard Rose's voice from downstairs call, "Your breakfast is ready, Dad," and Mr. Hudkins call back from the front room, "Okay, honey."

He dropped his dirty underwear and socks down the bathroom clothes chute, took a quick bath and put on his clean underwear and socks. Examining himself in the mirror, he wondered if it weren't about time he started shaving, but the blond fuzz on his face was so barely noticeable that he decided he could wait a while yet.

Back in the room he considered dropping his shirt down the chute too and going in just his skivvy shirt until it came in off the line, but he had worn it only once since the farmer's wife laundered it, and he decided it wasn't necessary.

When he got downstairs, he could hear a washing machine going in the basement. He glanced into the front room, saw it was empty, and noted by the clock on the fireplace mantel that it was only 8:00 A.M.

He went through the dining room into the kitchen, where he found Mr. Hudkins seated at the table eating bacon and eggs, and Rose, in a gingham housedress, frying bacon.

"Hi," she said over her shoulder, throwing him such a warm smile that he could feel his pulse rate increase. "Bacon and eggs will be up in a minute."

"Hi," he said, smiling back, then to her father, "Morning, sir."

"Morning, Hedge. Sit down."

Marion took a seat at the table.

"Mom's downstairs doing laundry," Rose said, her back to the table as she tended the frying bacon. "Barney up yet?"

"Not when I came down," Marion said.

Marion was nearly finished with breakfast when Barney came into the kitchen, wearing worn, multi-patched Levis, a T-shirt and tennis shoes.

"How come you didn't wake me up?" he asked Marion reproachfully.

"Figured you needed your beauty sleep," Marion told him with a grin.

Rose said to Barney, "You don't think you're wearing what you have on to the football game, do you?"

Flopping into a seat next to Marion, Barney said, "No, I'm gonna wear my cloth jacket too."

Rose directed an appeal to her father. "Make him change into some other pants, Dad."

Glancing at his son, Mr. Hudkins said, "Better change to school slacks and put on a shirt, Barney. We don't want your sister disgraced before her friends."

"Okay," Barney said resignedly. "But who ever heard of dressing up to go to a football game?"

Glancing at a watch, Mr. Hudkins said, "Game's at one, so we should leave here by twelve-thirty. We'll have an early lunch about eleven-thirty."

During lunch Marion learned that Mrs. Hudkins was not going with them to the football game. Apparently she had no interest in the sport, because he gathered that she never attended games.

Rose dressed for the game in a plain blue skirt, a fuzzy white sweater and penny loafers with bobby sox. Marion thought she looked lovely, but then he thought she looked lovely in anything. As befitted his status as a teacher, Mr. Hudkins wore a suit and necktie. Barney changed into gray slacks, a shirt and a zippered cloth jacket, but Marion noted that he still wore tennis shoes.

They drove the eight miles to Riverton in the Hudkins' 1936 Ford station wagon, which by its shiny appearance and purring engine seemed still to be in mint condition. Marion had somehow gotten the impression that Riverton was a large town, but he discovered it was large only in comparison to tiny Bidwell. A sign at the edge of town gave the population as 1,827.

The "stadium" was behind the ancient brick high school and consisted of a football field with a cinder track around it and wooden bleachers on one side. The bleachers had a total capacity of 500, but only about 300 fans were in attendance. They seemed evenly split between the Riverton section, which was the left half of the bleachers, and the visitors' section on the right.

There were three girl cheerleaders for each team, the Riverton ones in white with green R's on their sweaters, the visiting Westland cheerleaders in blue with gold W's. The team uniforms were the same color combinations.

Riverton High's band, a rather off-key group of ten brasses, a snare drum and a bass drum, was playing a spirited march as Marion and the three Hudkins made their way to seats. A lot of people in the stands waved to them, but the band was playing too loudly for any exchange of verbal greetings. Most of the wavers looked Marion over with frank but friendly curiosity.

Rose sat between Marion and her father, and Barney seated himself to Marion's left.

When the march ended, the Riverton cheerleaders led a cheer that went:

California grapefruit!
Texas cactus!
We play Westland
Just for practice!
YAAAY, RIVERTON!

At the last line all three cheerleaders leapt into the air with outstretched arms.

Riverton won the toss. Marion noted that for offense Riverton employed the traditional single wing, and that

Westland's defense formation was the standard 6-2-2-1.

On the kick-off play Riverton was stopped cold on its own twenty-yard line. By last down they were back to their own ten. The quarterback got off an excellent fifty-yard punt, but the Westland halfback who received it ran it back to the Riverton thirty-yard line.

Barney said glumly, "I told you. A slaughter."

Marion said, "They haven't scored yet, Ace."

Rose and her father glanced at each other, both grinning. Rose whispered, "Finally got somebody to call him Ace."

On the next play Riverton stopped the visitors on the line of scrimmage. A groan went up from the Westland section, while the Riverton fans cheered and shrieked and the bass drum thumped.

Throughout the first quarter and most of the second quarter the ball remained in Riverton territory, but Westland was unable to score. Then, with two minutes of the first half remaining, the Riverton quarterback faded back for a pass from behind his own goal line.

At first it looked as though he was never going to get it off. Holding the ball poised for throwing, he looked and looked for an open receiver as his blockers did their best to protect him from the charging enemy. Then, an instant before a Westland guard brought him down with a flying tackle, he threw the ball in a long, high spiral.

Coming up beneath the ball, running free, there suddenly appeared a player in a green-and-white uniform with the number 98 on his back. The ball began to arch downward, and he was reaching, straining toward it, and the crowd was going wild. From in front of him and behind blue-and-gold-clad players were converging, and 98 was still reaching, stretching his arms as far as they would go. And then he had the ball and was clasping it to his chest, and was neatly sidestepping a tackler and was stiff-arming another out of the way, and was racing like a deer with hounds yapping after it, past the fifty-yard line, was sidestepping a final tackler playing deep, then was in the clear and was uncatchable.

He crossed the goal line standing up, ritualistically

touched down the ball, and a huge groan went up from the right side of the stands as the left side went wild with cheering and horn blowing and the bass drum thumped and the Riverton cheerleaders did cartwheels.

Rose was hugging Marion and he was yelling, "Oh boy! Oh boy!" and Barney was alternately yelling and gaping in disbelief, and Mr. Hudkins was saying something no one could hear.

His teammates were hugging number 98, and the Riverton fans stopped cheering in order to give him a hand, and then the clamor died off enough to hear what Mr. Hudkins was trying to say.

"We'll have a lead at half time!" he exulted.

Marion said, "Hey, that number ninety-eight can catch *and* run, can't he?"

"Clay Carter," Rose said happily. "He's going in the Marines too."

The teams were lined up again, and the ball was snapped to a halfback, who positioned it on the ground for the Riverton quarterback to kick. It sailed precisely between the goal posts. Another cheer came from the Riverton fans and the bass drum boomed and the cheerleaders did more cartwheels.

"Extra point!" Mr. Hudkins exclaimed. "First one in two years!"

Rose and Barney and their father were all too excited to notice Marion's gradually subsiding excitement as he stared down at the field. A moment before he had been as elated as any other Riverton rooter, but now, as the teams lined up for a Riverton kick-off, a number of confusing thoughts began crowding through his mind.

There was the nostalgic memory of other days, when he was down on the field and the cheers from the stands were for him. There was the sad realization that some of the happy players might well be lying dead thousands of miles from home by this time next year. And there was the bitter thought that he, who had so desperately wanted to go overseas as a Marine was instead sitting here in someone else's uniform, pretending to be a war hero, when in fact by Marine Corps classification he was only an idiot.

He was going to have to tell Rose, he decided suddenly. Today, even if it destroyed what was growing between them, as he was sickly sure it would. But not until after the game. There was no point in ruining the game for her.

Turning to him, Rose said with sudden inspiration, "Hedge, Clay'd be just thrilled to meet you after the game."

"Sure, Rose," he said with a wan smile. "Sure."

Mr. Hudkins glanced past Rose at Marion, saw the expression on his face, and his own face sobered. Partially guessing what was bothering Marion, he looked down at the field again and said in a soft voice, "They'll all be going soon."

With time running out, Riverton naturally delayed as much as possible in the hope that the half would end before Westland could mount an offensive. The strategy worked, and when the half ended, the score remained 7-0 favor Riverton.

The band began playing an off-key arrangement of Glenn Miller's "In the Mood."

"Anybody feel like a hotdog and a Coke?" Mr. Hudkins asked, rising to his feet.

Instantly jumping up, Barney said, "I sure do."

Rose said to Marion, "I will if you do."

"I never refuse a dare," he said smiling at her. "Besides, I'm hungry."

Chapter 17

The refreshment booth was underneath the stands. Mr. Hudkins ordered and paid for four hotdogs and four Cokes. They carried them a short distance away from the milling crowd around the booth before stopping to consume them.

"Beautiful pass," Mr. Hudkins commented, his mind still on the first half. "Perfect spiral."

Barney said, "I still don't believe it. Almost as good as Johnny Elmore."

Everyone seemed to have left the stands, even those not wanting refreshments. That was understandable, because the only half-time entertainment was the band, and distance improved the enjoyment of its playing.

Passersby kept calling greetings to Mr. Hudkins, and he kept smiling and nodding to the greeters. Some of the greetings seemed meant to include Rose and Barney too, but Rose was oblivious to anything but Marion, and Barney was concentrating on his hotdog. Those ignored didn't seem to resent it, though. Most of them seemed amused by Barney's preoccupation and rather touched by Rose's.

Mr. Hudkins, Marion and Barney finished their hotdogs and Cokes and tossed their cups into a nearby trash can. Rose, nibbling and sipping more delicately, wasn't even half finished when Mr. Hudkins spotted someone in the crowd he wanted to speak to, took Barney by the arm and steered him in that direction.

Rose and Marion began idly drifting toward the aisle between the two sections of bleachers, Rose still carrying her Coke in one hand and her partially eaten hotdog in the other.

Suddenly Rose spotted three girls of about her own age just ahead, standing together and staring toward her and Marion. They too wore skirts and sweaters and bobby sox and loafers. She gave the girls only a fleeting look, then instinctively shifted her Coke to the same hand holding the hotdog and groped for Marion's right hand with her left.

Surprised but pleased, he clasped the small hand in his big one. She made an awkward attempt to take a bite of her hotdog without spilling her Coke, gave up and threw him a helpless look. He reached across to take the hotdog from her with his left hand and held it for her to bite.

"Umm," she said. "Thanks."

They came abreast of the three girls. Rose gave a gifted performance of being unaware of them standing there, all three of them overwhelmed by the sight of her holding hands with such a terrific Marine. She had Marion feed her another bite of hotdog.

The shortest of the three girls, a shapely but almost plump brunette, said, "Hi, Rose."

Glancing that way in simulated surprise, Rose said, "Oh, hi, Ruth Ellen."

The next tallest, and by far the prettiest of the three, an ash blonde, said, "Hi, Rose."

"Hi, Susan."

The third girl, also an ash blonde, but a little too thin, and stoop-shouldered in an attempt to disguise her five-foot-eight height, was stricken mute. Smiling at her, Rose said, "Hi, Jane."

She gave Rose a frozen smile, but made no reply. None of the girls so much as looked at Marion. He would have felt invisible if it had not been so apparent that they were so totally aware of him that actually they were hardly seeing Rose, even with their gazes fixed on her.

Having savored her moment of triumph, Rose was really too sweet-natured to drive it into the ground. Graciously she made introductions.

"Girls, this is Hedge—Corporal Hedgepeth. Hedge, Ruth Ellen Daugherty, Susan Ball and Jane Quinlan."

The plump brunette said, "Pleased to meet you." The pretty ash blonde said, "Hi, Hedge." The tall girl gazed at him in stunned silence.

"Hi, girls," Marion said, giving them an all-inclusive smile.

From a short distance away Private Danny Phelps watched the scene with bitter envy. Watching from the other direction, Barney elbowed his father's arm to get him to look too.

Rose said to the girls, "Hedge is staying at our place before he goes on to St. Louis."

"St. *Louis!*" the brunette said, as though it were Paris.

Marion said, "Thought I'd see some of the country, and I sure like this part."

The pretty girl said, "Well, it can't be our big, modern skyscrapers, so it must be the company." She and the brunette both giggled.

Pulling Marion on by the hand, Rose said, "Well, see you."

The girls started to move off too and collided with each other. Over his shoulder Marion said, "Nice meeting you all."

Both speaking at once, so that it was difficult to sort out the words, the short brunette and the pretty ash blonde said something that sounded like, "Bye, Hedge. Nice. See you, Rose. Meeting you."

The tall girl still said nothing, looking back over her shoulder, speechless with awe at the big, handsome Marine corporal. She bumped into Danny Phelps, who backed away and said in a grumpy voice, "Sorry."

Spectators were beginning to drift back to their seats, but the stands were still largely empty. It was therefore easy to pick out a familiar face from among the few seated fans. As they climbed toward their seats, Marion spotted a face he knew in the very highest row, clear over in the farthest corner next to the goal line. He came to a halt, looking that way, and because he had been courteously helping Rose along by the elbow, she stopped to look in the same direction.

Mr. Elmore was seated there, apart from everyone else,

gazing bleakly down at the players now running back onto the field.

Rose said with a sympathetic sigh, "His last game, Johnny Elmore made three touchdowns."

Marion looked away from the grieving face and exerted gentle pressure on Rose's elbow in signal to resume climbing.

A few minutes after they were seated, just as the two teams finished lining up for the kick-off, Rose's father rejoined them.

Then the kick-off came, and Marion's attention centered on the game.

During the third quarter Westland scored a touchdown, but failed to convert. Riverton held them scoreless during the fourth quarter, and game ended 7-6 for Riverton. The Riverton fans went wild.

As everyone got up to leave, Rose said, "I'd like Hedge to meet Clay, Dad."

"All right," Mr. Hudkins said. "Barney and I will wait at the car."

He and Barney moved off to the right. Rose and Marion descended straight downward, stepping from seat to seat, until they reached the cinder track encircling the football field. A crowd of wellwishers were around the Riverton players, who now all had either parkas or blankets wrapped around them against too quick cooling off.

One of the Riverton cheerleaders, a slim, freckled strawberry blonde with a pretty face, was hugging number 98. When she finally released him, Rose called to her, "Sylvia!"

The girl peered at her through the crowd of fans, then made her way through them over to Rose and Marion.

"This is Sylvia Carr, Hedge," Rose introduced. "Corporal Hedgepeth, Sylvia."

"Hi," the girl said, gazing at him with interest, but without the awe registered by the three girls he had met previously.

"Hi, Sylvia."

"Hedge wants to meet Clay," Rose said. "Think you could steer him over here?"

"You bet," the strawberry blonde said, turning to make her way back through the crowd.

Rose said, "Sylvia is Clay's girl friend. She must be proud."

"She ought to be," Marion said.

Chapter 18

The crowd of fans was beginning to break up when Sylvia got back to Clay Carter, and some of the players were starting to head for the showers. Sylvia said something to Clay, he glanced toward Rose and Marion, then he and the girl both came over.

As Rose made introductions, Sylvia stood beaming with pride at Clay. He was a square-faced, rather good-looking boy of good size, as tall as Marion, and at the moment having unnaturally wide shoulders because of the shoulder pads beneath his jersey. He wore a parka around his shoulders and his football helmet dangled from his left hand by the chin strap.

As the two shook hands, Clay said with the respect usually accorded only older persons, "It's an honor to meet you."

Marion smiled at him. "Some game you played."

"I'll say," Rose put in. "We haven't beaten Westland in eight years."

Pleased, but made self-conscious by the compliment, Clay eyed Marion's ribbons and made an apologetic gesture. "Kid stuff, really. Just a game."

"Hedge used to play too," Rose said. "End."

"Really?" Clay said, looking him up and down. "You've got an end's build."

There was an awkward silence, finally broken by Clay blurting, "I'm joining the Marines soon as I graduate. It's the best branch."

"Sure is," Marion agreed.

"Think they'll have me?" Clay asked with a touch of

worry. "I'd hate to have to go in the Army. Anybody can do that."

Anybody, Marion thought wryly. Then he had a horrible thought. Suppose he was too much of an idiot even to make it in the Army?

The thought shook him enough so that instead of the reassurance he meant to give, he could only manage to say, "That's right."

After another awkward pause, Clay said, "We knew you were up in the stands."

Raising his eyebrows, Marion asked, "How's that?"

Grinning, Clay said, "Can't keep secrets in small towns. Coach told us you were here. Hope it doesn't sound corny, but it kind of gave everybody a lift. You know, with Johnny Elmore being gone and all."

Again he had inspired memories of Johnny Elmore, Marion thought, hating the part he was playing even more. He said a trifle disjointedly, "I met Mr. Elmore. Bought me breakfast. Real nice man."

"Sure is. Well, better grab a shower." He looked at the ribbons again. "We're real proud you came to see us."

As Clay and Sylvia moved away together, Marion gazed after the football player, his guilt at the lie he was living suddenly overwhelming him. Turning to Rose, he braced himself and said, "Johnny Elmore, he must have been some kind of guy. I don't think people should—"

"Should what?" she asked when he broke off, puzzled by his tone.

He took a deep breath and expelled it slowly. "Look, Rose, there's something I ought to tell you before——"

She interrupted him because at that moment she happened to glance through the spaces between the bleacher tiers toward the parking lot beyond, and caught sight of her father standing next to the station wagon, motioning them to come on.

"Dad's signaling, Hedge. We better hurry."

Almost in anguish, Marion said, "Rose—"

"But I'll tell you something right now," she said, grabbing his hand and pulling him toward the aisle between the two sets of bleachers. "I'm proud, Hedge. I'm so proud of you, I could bust."

She looked up into his eyes as they moved hand in hand along the aisle. And there was no way at that moment that he could tell her.

On the way home Barney turned around in the front seat to say to Marion, sitting with Rose in the center seat, and said, "You know you can't say war's *all* bad."

"Go on, child philosopher," Mr. Hudkins said dryly.

"It brought Hedge here," Barney said with triumph.

Rose started to smile agreement, but then the smile faded. "He has to go again."

With thirteen-year-old concern for the moment only, this seemed not to have occurred to Barney. Momentarily he looked concerned, but instantly brightened again. "Maybe he'll come back," he said with hope.

Rose glanced sidewise at Marion for confirmation of the hope. He summoned a smile, but he was unable to look at her. She seemed to take it as a promise, because she squeezed his hand.

That evening Marion took Rose to the movie. They sat near the rear and held hands during the half dozen shorts preceding the feature film. They contined to hold hands halfway through "Dark Victory," but as the eventual tragic ending became more and more inevitable, Rose dropped Marion's hand to dig a handkerchief from her purse and clutch it. Thereafter she occasionally touched the handkerchief to her eyes.

Marion also started to become deeply affected by the unfolding story, but tradition decreed that a man in Marine uniform show no emotion over a mere movie. At the farewell scene at the car, when Bette Davis asked bravely, "Have I been a good wife?" Rose began to weep. Marion felt his eyes misting, but manfully blinked away the tears.

When George Brent drove off, with Bette Davis calling after him, "Hurry home!" Rose had to stuff the wadded handkerchief into her mouth to keep from sobbing aloud. Marion dropped a comforting arm about her shoulder, but she was too wrapped up in the screen tragedy even to notice.

The music built as Miss Davis retired to her room and the maid covered her with a blanket. When the actress said, "I don't want to be disturbed," it was too much for Rose. The sound of sobbing came from her. Marion, clenching his teeth in order to hold back his own grief, gave her shoulder a comforting squeeze.

When they came from the theater, Rose wiped her reddened eyes and gave Marion an apologetic look. He was tempted to make some joking remark, such as, "She didn't really die, because I read she's making another movie," but he sensed she wouldn't appreciate the humor. Instead he just said, "Pretty sad story."

"Yes," she said. Putting away her handkerchief, she said bravely, "Want to stop by the Oasis for a Coke or something?"

"I thought it closed at eight," he said.

"Ten on Saturdays, and it's only about a quarter to."

"All right," he agreed.

They crossed the street and went into the café. The place was empty of customers, but through the opening above the service counter they could see the cook Charlie cinder-blocking the grill.

As they took seats at the counter, Rose said, "He must have let Thelma go home early."

Hearing her, the cook glanced through the opening, and a resigned expression formed on his face. "My nice clean grill, and now two cheeseburgers."

Marion looked at Rose, who shook her head. "Just a Coke."

"You're in luck," Marion said to the cook. "Just a Coke and a coffee."

Charlie came from the kitchen. Noting Rose's reddened eyes, he frowned and asked, "What's the matter, honey?"

"Bette Davis died," Marion said.

Charlie looked unbelieving. "The actress?"

"In the movie across the street," Marion explained.

"Oh." Looking at Rose, he said, "Just a movie, Rose."

Then, trying to cheer her up, he said, "Couple of cheeseburgers, huh? On the house."

Pulling out his remaining dollar and a half, Marion laid it on the counter and said firmly, "I'm paying this time, thanks."

Rose shook her head at Charlie. "Just a small Coke."

Marion shrugged. "And coffee," he said, picking up his dollar, but letting the half dollar lie.

As Charlie squirted Coke syrup into a glass, Marion, attempting to get Rose out of her depressed mood, glanced around and said, "Nice place here."

"Want to buy it?" Charlie asked. "Fifty bucks? Forty-five?"

Marion grinned, and after a moment Rose grinned too, cheering both Marion and the cook. Charlie ran carbonated water into the glass, added ice and a straw and set it before Rose. He drew Marion's coffee, set it before him, looked at the half dollar lying on the counter for a time, and finally reluctantly rang up a dime. As he put the forty cents change in front of Marion, Private Danny Phelps came in.

Seating himself at the other counter, catercorner to Rose and Marion, he said, "Hi."

Marion said, "What say, Army?" and Rose said without much enthusiasm, "Hi, Danny."

"Coffee," the Army private said to Charlie.

"On the wagon, huh?" the cook said "No more chocolate Cokes?"

Ignoring him, Danny said to Marion, "Know how many of our tanks Rommel wiped out in North Africa?"

"A lot, I heard," Marion said.

Charlie set a cup of coffee in front of the Army private. Danny started to spoon sugar into it, his gaze fixed on Marion. "Course my size is really an advantage. They can train me as a tank gunner, then put me in B-Seventeens. You can do that, you know. Go from the Army to the Air Corps."

With a pained look on his face Charlie drew himself a cup of coffee, apparently as an antidote to Danny's blather.

Danny said, "That belly-turret on the seventeen. Can't wear a chute, so you got to get in and out from outside. If you crash-land, well, know how they get you out?"

"How?" Marion asked curiously.

"With a hose."

Looking faintly ill, Rose said, "Oh, Danny, for heaven's sake!"

Danny gave her a bare glance before returning his attention to Marion. "Hey, Marine, ever been in a plane?"

"Nope."

"Met a captain who took me up," Danny said importantly. "Loop-the-loop and everything, and not a bit sick. Course to get in the planes you got to have a high IQ."

Rose sucked the last of her Coke, looked at Marion's nearly empty coffee cup and said, "Can we go, Hedge?"

Frowning at Danny Phelps, Marion asked, "What was that about IQ?"

"Just a fact. They give tests. And different people get different scores."

The boy was beginning to get under Marion's skin. Sensing this, and not even dreaming that Marion's ordinary reaction to needling was merely verbal anger, Charlie tried to sidetrack the Marine corporal from devouring Danny by turning the whole thing into a joke.

He said to Danny, "Forget it far as he's concerned, because he's got no IQ. He said I got a nice place here, wants to buy it. But I don't know. The thrill of getting up at four in the morning to make pancakes. The suspense of eggs over easy."

Marion and Rose both started to smile, but Danny didn't get it. He gazed at the cook without understanding.

Turning to Marion, Charlie said, "You sure you're man enough for French toast? Those medals don't fool me. I'd like to see you face to face with lumpy mashed potatoes."

Rose erupted into laughter. Marion started to chuckle. Danny finally got the joke, but he didn't think it was funny.

"Charlie, we were having a serious conversation," he complained.

Cocking an eyebrow at Danny, the cook asked, "Know what else he said? He likes the town." Turning back to Marion, he said, "Came here ten years ago for my health. It's never been worse."

Marion's chuckle turned to a barely controlled laugh. The cook said to him, "See the football game today?"

When Marion gave him a laughter-weak nod, he said, "That's the excitement for the year."

Now laughing almost uncontrollably, Rose said, "Oh, Charlie!"

"Unless you want to watch a train go by," Charlie said, now really warming up. "Or watch old Sam Willis. He does some job with a toothpick after roast beef."

This time even Private Phelps joined in the laughter.

Charlie said to Rose, "Want another Coke?" He glanced at Marion. "More coffee?"

"Thanks, Charlie, but no," Rose said. "We'd better be going."

"Yeah," Marion said lightly. "She roped me into church tomorrow."

He and Rose both got up from their stools and started for the door.

"Church!" Danny said, making it sound like a place for sissies.

"Wouldn't hurt you," Charlie growled at him. "Maybe stop you from bulling so much."

The door closed behind Marion and Rose.

Chapter 19

The Hudkins had just closed the door of their bedroom when they heard Rose and Marion come in. As they undressed for bed, they listened to their daughter and their house guest come up the stairs, conversing quietly. Because of a space below the bedroom door, where Tom Hudkins had once planed off too much when the door was sticking, they could clearly hear the conversation.

The couple paused at the top of the stairs and they heard Rose say, "Sorry I cried, but it was a sad movie."

"I almost cried too."

"You?" Rose scoffed. "I don't believe that."

"I don't mean in the movie. I mean at Charlie's sad story."

They heard their daughter giggle. "Isn't he a scream?"

There was a long silence then, eventually broken by Rose saying softly, "See you in the morning."

"Yeah, good night."

Moments later they heard the door to Rose's room, next to theirs, open and close, then the door to Barney's room up the hall also open and close.

They had not said a word to each other while getting ready for bed, because both had been listening to the conversation in the hallway. Now they exchanged sheepish glances, slightly ashamed of themselves for eavesdropping. Tom Hudkins, wearing pajamas, went into the bathroom to brush his teeth. Helen Hudkins sat before her dressing table mirror in a nightgown and began brushing her hair.

When the water stopped running in the bathroom, so

that she could be heard, Helen said, "We'll have to see that movie."

Tom emerged from the bathroom and came over to stand behind her, watching her brush her hair. Glancing at his reflection in the mirror, she saw the thoughtful frown on his face.

"Something wrong?" she asked.

"Just thinking about Hedge."

Finishing her brushing, she laid down the brush and turned around on the dressing table bench to face him. "What about him?"

He ran distracted fingers through his hair. "That uniform. Do you know what it means?"

"Why, Marines," she said, surprised at the question.

"I mean the shoulder patch."

"Oh, the skull. His outfit insigne, I assume."

"He's a Raider, a special Marine outfit that was written up in *Look*. They're—well, special." He paused, searching for words to explain without giving her the impression he thought Hedge was some kind of monster. Eventually he gave up and simply said, "Barney tells me he's killed men."

Getting up from the bench, she went over to seat herself on the edge of the bed. "Well, in war—you mean how can he still be so—so innocent?"

"Look so innocent," he corrected. "Maybe he was before going overseas, but a man doesn't live through a nightmare and come back the same."

She gazed up at him, knowing that his concern wasn't really for Hedge, but for Rose. He was having typical fatherly worries.

She said, "I don't think he's kissed her yet."

"Neither do I. But you know what I was thinking when she brought him home?"

"Same thing I was, probably."

Sighing, he plopped down on the edge of the bed beside her. "I liked him right off, understand. But I was thinking, he's only a boy on the outside. He's seen things most men never even see, because you grow up fast in war, if you manage to survive at all." There was a long pause before he continued, "Probably stopped in Honolulu on his way back. I mean prostitution."

Looking at him, she nodded agreement. He was slightly shocked that she wasn't in the least shocked. Again he distractedly ran fingers through his hair.

"Feel like a damn fool," he said. "Been treating our daughter like a lady, and I'm finding fault."

"Maybe he's had enough of the other kind of girls," she said equably. "Tom, all the old ways won't die."

They were both really skirting the issue, she realized, all at once facing it squarely in her own mind, although she would never be able to bring herself to discuss it openly with her husband. What they were both concerned about was the thought of their daughter, sometime, somewhere, losing her virginity to an experienced boy. They were discussing Hedge only because he was the most immediate danger.

The thought set her to thinking back to her own youth, when her parents must have had similar worries about her. She said reflectively, "Remember when we were courting? The stories out of Chicago and New York?"

He looked at her. "You mean bathtub gin? Wild parties?"

She smiled. "Fast women smoking in the street."

He smiled back at her. "Flappers. The Charleston."

A faint glint appeared in her eyes. "Ever wish you'd been there?"

"No," he said promptly, then grinned hugely and amended it to, "Yes."

She cocked an eyebrow at him. "With me?"

"Only with you," he assured her.

She giggled. "We'd have been out of place."

He shrugged. "Just get a room at the Waldorf, and take the phone off the hook."

They looked at each other, and each saw that the conversation had kindled a response in the eyes of the other. Taking her into his arms, he kissed her deeply, at the same time forcing her backward onto the bed.

She broke the kiss to say urgently, "Light. The light."

He reached to switch off the bedside lamp, plunging

the room into darkness. Slipping off and kicking aside his pajama bottoms, but leaving on the tops, he felt for her and slipped up her nightgown. Their lovemaking was always in darkness, never completely naked, as had been seemly during the era when they were first married.

In the next room, lying on her back in the darkness, thinking of Hedge, Rose heard the faint rhythmic sound of creaking bedsprings through the wall, and knew that her parents were making love. Putting the knuckle of a forefinger between her teeth, she stared up at the ceiling, wondering what it would be like with Hedge. Many times before she had heard the creaking springs and had wondered what it was like for her parents. This was the first time she had ever thought about having it happen to her with a specific boy, and the thought flooded her with a strange feeling of warmth.

Marion was also lying in bed on his back, staring upward in the darkness at the underside of the upper bunk and thinking of Rose. He was absolutely going to have to tell her the truth about himself, he thought. But the question was when? He had already committed himself to stay over one more day, but he had decided he would definitely leave Monday morning.

The time to tell her was just before he left, he decided. It meant one more day of masquerade, but also one more day of happiness.

He went to sleep on that thought.

The next morning at breakfast he made it clear to everyone that he would be leaving the following morning.

Mrs. Hudkins asked, "How long will you have at home?"

"Week, ten days. Leave myself enough time to hitchhike back to Dago before my thirty days are up."

"Will you be coming back this way?" Rose asked.

There was no point in adding to the lies already told by holding out hope for something that couldn't be. Without looking at her, he said, "Southern route's a lot faster. Down through Oklahoma and Texas and so on, along Route Sixty-six."

"Oh," Rose said, disappointed.

Barney said, "Don't guess they'll be sending you back over again, will they, Hedge?"

"I don't have much to say about that."

Rose looked at him from eyes suddenly grown enormous. "I didn't know you had to go back," she said, almost in a whisper.

"Didn't say I had to," Marion said. "Just said I didn't have much to say about it, one way or the other."

He probably would be going over, he thought, if they took him into the Army. Not going over *again,* but just over. He hoped no one would ask what he thought his chances were of being shipped out, because he would have to tell still another lie by assessing them as slim, and he was becoming tired of lies.

Mr. Hudkins saved him the trouble of lying by making an affirmative statement instead of asking a question. "They wouldn't send you back. You've done your part.

Rose looked relieved by the statement. Marion made no comment.

Church was from eleven until noon. The Hudkins and their house guest sat in the front row. Mrs. Hudkins and Rose wore their best dresses, hats and gloves. Mr. Hudkins wore his pin-stripe suit and Barney his blue serge one. But as they made their ways to their seats, all eyes in the congregation were on Marion's uniform.

It was a Congregational church, and Marion wasn't quite sure just what that was. The service seemed not a great deal different from that of other Protestant churches he had attended. There were some readings from the Bible, some hymns, some prayers, an offering was collected, then the minister delivered a sermon.

There was one difference from anything Marion had ever seen in another church, though. The minister, whose name was the Reverend Cobb, announced he was dedicating his sermon to the United States Marines.

Marion suspected the dedication was impromptu, occurring to the minister only after he spotted the Marine uniform in the front row. Aside from a reference to the famed Marine action in Tripoli in the early 1800s, which also seemed to be impromptu, the sermon had only an extremely remote bearing on the Marine Corps. Its theme was the ancient ecclesiastical concept of "just war" as opposed to "immoral war."

According to the Reverend Cobb, the concept had been the subject of considerable ecclesiastical debate during the Middle Ages, without the matter ever being clearly resolved. At one point, the minister said, the Pope decreed that under certain circumstances it was possible for both warring parties to have God on their sides. That, of course, was ridiculous, he assured the congregation, but it *was* possible for even something as horrible as war to be just in the eyes of God. Whereupon he proceeded to establish by Biblical precedent that in the present worldwide conflict, God was definitely on the side of the Allies.

Since the Marines were involved in that conflict, conceivably the sermon at least remotely concerned them, but the connection remained unclear to Marion.

After the service it was necessary for him to meet and shake hands with everyone in the congregation, which it seemed to him must have included at least half the population of the town. The last one he met was the Reverend Cobb, and that was because the minister had stationed himself in the doorway to greet parishioners on the way out. He was a large, plump man with a benign smile and soft white hands, both of which he used when shaking hands. He gripped Marion's hand with his right and simultaneously squeezed it with his left, while telling him that he was honored to have Marion attend his church.

Marion told him he had enjoyed his sermon.

Marion and Rose finally broke away and descended the church steps. Barney, who had long since escaped from the church, was sitting on the curbside front fender of the Hudkins station wagon, feet dangling, talking to a couple of boys his own age. Rose's mother and father were still talking to the minister. It was the first time that day that Marion and Rose had found themselves alone, or at least far enough separated from others for private conversation.

Pausing on the sidewalk at the bottom of the steps,

Marion said, "Whew! I'm telling you, Rose, that's the worst time I ever had in church."

"You mean Pastor Cobb dedicating the sermon to the United States Marines?"

Grinning, Marion said, "Surprised he didn't have everybody sing 'From the Halls of Montezuma'."

Laughing, she grabbed onto his arm and squeezed it. The caress sent a shiver through him, but it also slightly embarrassed him. He glanced around to see if anyone was observing them, failed to find any eyes looking their way, and was relieved. He looked up at the steep hill beginning just beyond the edge of town and rising to the plateau where the Japanese detention camp was.

Following his gaze, she said, "We call it a mountain, but it really doesn't come up to the Rockies."

"It's a nice mountain," he assured her.

"Want to climb it?"

He looked down into her face. "Someday," he said in a tone that made it a promise. It meant he was coming back to her.

Neither dared speak for a long time. They just stood there, she clinging to his arm, silently pledging their commitment. Finally she sighed and said, "You'll go tomorrow," and he said, "Guess so."

Chapter 20

On Sundays the Hudkins had dinner after church instead of in the evening. It was two in the afternoon before they finished eating, and nearly three before Mrs. Hudkins and Rose finished the dishes.

When she finally came from the kitchen, Rose suggested a walk to Marion.

"Sure," he said, eyeing her high-heeled shoes dubiously. "But don't you think you ought to change into something easier to walk in?"

"I planned to," she told him. "Be right back."

She went upstairs, and when she returned, she had not only changed into saddle shoes, but had changed from the dress she had worn to church into a skirt and sweater.

As they walked hand-in-hand in the direction of town, Rose said, "You've seen the river?"

Marion nodded. "Little woodchuck. We stood there looking at each other."

"Deer come down too."

"Water's like ice, I bet," Marion said. "But, boy, those trout sure must like it."

They reached Main Street and turned left. Rose said, "I like the hills too. Smell of all the flowers."

Gazing up at the hill beyond the other end of town, Marion said, "This sure is fine country."

They had reached the street crossing Main at the Oasis Café and the sheriff's sub-station across from the restaurant. Pausing, Rose asked, "Would a Marine pick a girl some flowers?"

"This one will," Marion said promptly.

She steered him across the street and past the sub-station along the graveled road leading in the direction of the river. When they reached the path Marion had taken the other day, they had to go in single file. He let her go first.

At the stepping-stone bridge over the rapids, he took the lead, holding onto her hand and helping her from rock to rock. When they stepped onto the flower-covered bank on the other side, she was flushed and laughing from the excitement of the crossing.

Glancing around at the expanse of yellow flowers, he asked, "These the ones you had in mind?"

"Yes," she said. "But not now. On the way back."

She took the lead again, climbing the path alongside the stream. When they reached the spot where he had rested the other day, just below the crest of the rise, she sank onto a grassy plot alongside the path. He sat next to her. For a time neither said anything, merely resting and regaining their breaths from the exertion of the climb.

Finally they looked at each other and smiled. He said, "Rose, I'm going to say something."

Her smile faded, to be replaced by a waiting expression.

Resting his left palm on the ground behind her, so that her shoulder was nestled against his, he said, "I have this uncle of mine, and he always says this: 'I love my wife, and my kids, and all my friends, and I wouldn't trade my job for anything in the world, and if I had it to do all over again, I'd do it just the same. But I'll never forget a brown-haired girl who served me coffee in Upper Sandusky, Ohio."

Instead of giggling, as he expected, her eyes misted. Turning her head toward his, their lips came within an inch of each other. His heart began to pound. Then his arms were about her, and her arms were about his neck, and they were kissing.

After a time she drew back her head, eyes closed, and sighed. He blurted out what he had been thinking for days. "I love you, Rose."

They kissed again, thoroughly, but with the innocence of new love, without passion. When their lips finally parted, he said, "I'll write. No matter where, or what."

"I'll write back every day," she said.

She laid her head on his shoulder and he held her, his thoughts churning, guilt flooding him because he had meant to confess his lie before confessing his love, and now it was all wrong because it was the lie that had made her return his love, and when he told her now, her love would probably die again.

On the verge of telling her right now, simply blurting it out, he panicked and instead reached out for a subject having nothing to do with either love or confession.

Dropping his hand palm down on the ground behind her again, he looked up toward the crest of the rise and said, "Hey, isn't that camp right up there?"

Puzzled, she lifted her head from his shoulder to look that way, then looked into his face.

He said, "I saw it that first afternoon I was here."

Still puzzled, and not really interested, she merely continued to look into his face. But he clung to the subject like a drowning man clinging to a life preserver.

"How'd you feel when they came?" he asked.

Seeing he was determined to pursue the subject, she straightened away from him and hugged her knees. "Mad, I guess, like most of the town." She frowned sidewise at him. "But, Hedge, you shouldn't think about them. They're not soldiers."

He hadn't really been thinking about them but only wildly grabbing for a new subject. But now he did, and had to agree with her. "I know," he said. "Old men and women, and kids barely walking. And Boy Scouts, if you can believe that."

Rose nodded sadly, beginning to become interested in the subject. "My dad's got into a lot of arguments. He says we'll be sorry for what we did to them."

He considered this, not knowing whether he agreed or not. "Well, they did bomb Pearl Harbor," he said finally. "And killed Mr. Elmore's boy."

She gave her head an impatient shake. Gesturing toward the plateau above them, she said, "It wasn't them. I know it's hard for you, Hedge, but it wasn't a single one of them."

It wasn't, of course, he thought. He thought about it some more but still could come to no conclusion. Finally he just gave up. Pushing himself to his feet, he held out a hand to help her up.

"Let's go back," he suggested.

As she came to her feet, she said, "You better go first downhill; in case I slip, you can catch me."

He went down the hill fast, forcing her almost to run behind him. When they reached the edge of the yellow field of flowers, he paused to look back and she sank gracefully to the ground, emitting a stage sigh of exhaustion. He walked back to stand over her, looking down.

"You walk so fast," she said.

"Used to it, I guess."

She gazed up at him, unsmiling now, her expression half guarded, half waiting, the look of a girl prepared to be made into a woman. The message was so clear that he felt instant reaction in the region of his groin.

The moment of truth had finally come, he realized, torn between the sudden surge of passion and despair. His plan to put off confession until morning was now impossible. Declaring his love without first confessing the lie had been bad enough. But physically taking her under false pretenses would be unforgivable.

In agony he pressed both hands against his chest, to the glory of his uniform.

"I can't," he said huskily. "Rose, this isn't me."

She stared up into his tormented face without understanding.

"I'm not a Marine," he said. "I tried to be, but the harder I tried, the worse it got. Whatever it was, it just wasn't in me."

Her expression became confused and a little frightened. Not frightened for herself, but for him.

"Don't you understand?" he said almost wildly. "They kicked me out of boot camp. They gave us blue suits and a cap. Called us Baby Blue Marines, said we were idiots, and that we should go home and get drafted by the Army or Navy or just be Four-F."

"But your stories," she whispered, her eyes pleading

with him to salvage something of himself for her, not to destroy her completely.

He began pacing back and forth in front of her. "Oh, they were real. I *was* in boot camp. But that Andy with the white hair I told you about. I met him in a Los Angeles bar, not in the jungle." He halted to point a thumb at his uniform jacket. "This is his. I was in the bar, waiting for a bus, and he came in and started buying me Scotch whiskeys. We were just talking. Anyway, I got sick and went out in the alley, and I guess he knocked me out and took my clothes and papers, and left his uniform all folded up next to me, and left me two dollars."

Beginning to comprehend, Rose released her indrawn breath. "He deserted!"

He spread his palms in a plea for her understanding, not for what he had done, but for Andy. "They were sending him back. He was only *twenty*, and already an old man."

Her gaze moved to his ribbons, and she looked as though she were going to cry.

"I couldn't turn him in," he said miserably. "They would have *hung* him. It wasn't his fault, you see. He just *couldn't* go back."

Rose wiped away a tear with the back of her hand. "Even after what he did to you?"

He made a dismissing gesture. "Anyway, I had to wear something. I just started thumbing a ride."

She took a deep breath, wiped her other eye with the back of her other hand and fixed her gaze on his face. "Are you from that little town near St. Louis you said?" she demanded.

He nodded, then said dispiritedly, "But it's not like I said to your sheriff. I've got family. They were so proud I was gonna be a Marine, like my dad." Sinking to his knees before her, he said, "But now I've got to go home and tell 'em, 'Okay, I'm sorry, but I didn't have whatever it takes to be a Marine.' If they don't like it, well, too bad."

She gazed into his eyes, suffering with him.

"But your dad and mom and Barney, and Mr. Elmore.

I don't want to tell them. I like 'em too much. But I will if you say, and take whatever they say back."

She shook her head, her eyes squeezed tightly shut.

He said hopefully, "When I write, I could say I got put in a special branch of—wherever I end up."

Opening her eyes, she said, "Yes. I don't want them to know. For their sakes."

He felt a bare touch of hope. It grew to disbelieving certainty when she reached out a delicate forefinger to touch his chest, then run it along his combat ribbons.

"Dark green wool," she said wistfully. "Pretty colored ribbons."

"Not mine," he said, shaking his head. "I could get put in prison."

"No. When they find out, they'll just see what I do. What we all do."

She moved forward to put her arms about his neck. He crushed her to him.

"I'll always love you," he said brokenly.

She leaned backward, drawing him with her, yielding herself in the graceful untaught manner of innocence unemcumbered by inhibition. Gently he moved onto her.

"Oh, darling," she said. "It's all right. It's going to be all right."

Chapter 21

At 4:00 A.M. Main Street in Bidwell was deserted. Since the village had no street lights, and there was no moon, the street was pitch dark. But suddenly it was brightly lighted by two sets of headlights descending the steep hill to the west of town.

The first vehicle was an Army jeep with a sergeant behind the wheel, a captain seated next to him, and two helmeted privates armed with rifles in the back seat. Jammed into the weapons carrier following the jeep were ten more helmeted enlisted men with rifles, two in front and eight in back.

The vehicles moved through town to the far end of the business section, swung left and parked diagonally side by side in front of the sheriff's sub-station. The captain swung himself out of the jeep between the two vehicles. He was a lean, swarthy man of about thirty with narrow features and a head too small for his body, with the result that his helmet gave him a kind of turtle-like look. He was armed with a holstered .45 caliber automatic.

"Wait here," he said, addressing both the sergeant driver of the jeep and the corporal driver of the weapons carrier. He had a strong Brooklyn accent.

He went over to pound on the door of the sub-station. After a time a light went on inside, the door cracked open and a thin, elderly man in bare feet, with trousers pulled on over his long underwear, looked out.

"Sheriff Wenzel?" the captain asked.

"Naw, I'm just the local deputy," the elderly man said. "Jake Rollins. Sheriff's office is over at the county seat."

The captain pushed the door open farther, forcing Deputy Rollins to move aside, and stepped indoors. The sub-station was furnished meagerly. There was a desk with a telephone on it, a couple of extra chairs against the wall, a single filing cabinet, and a bulletin board with several "wanted" posters tacked to it. To the left at the rear of the room the barred door of a single cell, empty, stood open. To the right another doorway with an ordinary wooden door presumably led to living quarters.

In a sour voice the captain said, "Better get your sheriff over here. I'm Captain Bittman, the new commander of the relocation camp above town. There's been an escape."

Deputy Rollins scratched his head, pushed the door closed and went over to the phone. The number he dialed rang for a long time before a sleepy male voice finally said, "Hello."

The deputy said, "Sheriff? Jake Rollins. Captain in charge of the Jap camp above town's here. Says there's been an escape. I'll let you talk to him."

He handed the phone to the captain. In his strong Brooklyn accent the Army officer said, "Captain Bittman, Sheriff. We've had three men escape, same three that took off about six weeks ago, when Captain Wheeler was camp commander. Only this time they're armed with M-1 rifles."

"And ammo?" the sheriff asked sharply.

"Uh-huh."

"Suppose you want a posse," Sheriff Wenzel said without much enthusiasm.

"I understand you raised one for my predecessor, Captain Wheeler."

"All right," the sheriff said resignedly. "Let me talk to Deputy Rollins again."

The captain handed the phone back to the old man. "Yeah, Sheriff?" the deputy said.

"I'll be over there in a half hour," the sheriff told him. "Meantime start recruiting a posse. You know who to call. Also phone Charlie Fox and get him to open the Oasis, so the posse can wake up on coffee, or have some breakfast if they want. Tell Charlie he can bill the county for what he serves."

"Okay, Sheriff," Rollins said. "I'll take care of it."

At 4:20 A.M. the Hudkins' phone rang. Since it was downstairs in the entry hall, it was some moments before Tom Hudkins got down to answer it. He caught it on the tenth ring.

When he said, "Hello," the caller said, "Charlie Fox, Mr. Hudkins. Those same three nisei have escaped again, and this time they grabbed M-1 rifles before they took off. Jake Rollins is getting up a posse, and he wants you."

"All right. Where and when?"

"The Oasis, soon as you can get there. I'll need Rose to help. Will you tell her I'll be by for her in fifteen minutes?"

"All right."

"Hedge is gone by now, I imagine," Charlie said.

"No, plans to leave in the morning."

"Oh," the restaurant owner said in a pleased voice. "Better bring him along then."

Helen Hudkins was sitting up in bed with the light on when her husband reentered the bedroom. "What is it?" she asked.

"Escape from the internment camp. Same three boys, only this time they're armed." He stripped off his pajamas and started to dress. "Posse's gathering at the Oasis, and Charlie Fox is coming by for Rose in fifteen minutes. Better go get her up."

Jumping from bed, she slipped a robe on over her nightgown, shoved her feet into slippers and ran to the room next door. He finished dressing before she returned, and went up the hall to Barney's room.

Marion was awakened from sound sleep by a soft knock on the door. It took him a few moments to orient himself, because he had been dreaming he was back in the idiots' barracks in San Diego. The congested breathing of the boy in the upper bunk, who still suffered from his cold, reminded him of where he was.

The knock came again before he could roll out and get to the door. Because he was in his underwear, and he assumed the knocker was Rose, he cracked it open only wide enough to peer out. When he saw the glint of Mr. Hudkins' spectacles in the dim hallway light, he opened it wide.

Mr. Hudkins whispered, "Get dressed, Hedge."

"What's wrong?" Marion asked, also whispering.

"Don't wake Barney."

"What's wrong?" Marion repeated, trying to whisper more softly.

"Escape," Mr. Hudkins whispered back, and turned to walk away rapidly.

Marion stared after him until he reached the stairway and disappeared down it. He hadn't the faintest idea of what Rose's father had been talking about, but it had sounded urgent. Leaving the door open, he dressed by the light from the hall. He put on his full uniform, including the jacket, except for the cap, which he folded and tucked into his belt.

Easing the door closed behind him so as not to waken Barney, he went down the hall to the main bathroom to brush his teeth before going downstairs. Both Rose's bedroom door and her parents' bedroom door were standing open, he noted, indicating that all three were probably downstairs. But as he started down the stairs, he heard a dresser drawer close in Mr. and Mrs. Hudkins' room. Apparently Rose's mother was still upstairs.

A light was burning in the lower hall, and another was burning in the kitchen. Marion went through the dining room into the kitchen. Mr. Hudkins, wearing a tan checkered mackinaw and a felt hat, was loading a Winchester lever-action deer rifle. A bolt-action Remington rifle, presumably already loaded, lay on the table.

Glancing at the wall clock, Marion saw it was twenty minutes of five. He asked, "What escape?"

"Three nisei," Mr. Hudkins said. "Ones who tried just six weeks ago. This time they made it."

Marion frowned. Glancing around the kitchen, he asked "Rose?"

"Oasis, with the soldiers, to get the coffee up."

Finishing loading the Winchester, Mr. Hudkins put

it on the table next to the Remington. Looking at the two rifles, Marion asked, "What for?"

"Decoration, I hope. But they've got M-1's." Gesturing to the rifles, he said, "Take your pick."

After the barest hesitation, Marion chose the Remington because it was bolt action. It wasn't a slide bolt, like the M-1's, but it looked easier to figure out than the lever-action gun. He had never in his life handled a lever-action gun.

Mr. Hudkins picked up the other gun, levered the chamber partially open and peered into it to see if there was a shell in the chamber. Marion was standing near enough to him to see that the chamber was empty. When Mr. Hudkins let it stay that way, Marion concluded with some relief that he didn't want shells in the chambers. He pulled back the bolt of his own gun far enough to see the chamber was empty, then pushed it forward again.

Carrying his rifle at trail position, Mr. Hudkins led the way from the room. Holding his with the muzzle pointing downward at an angle, Marion followed. With his free hand he pulled his folded cap from his belt and positioned it on his head.

Mrs. Hudkins, wearing a dressing robe over a nightgown, was standing by the front door, a red hunting cap in her hand.

She said, "Morning, Hedge."

"Morning, Mrs. Hudkins," he said politely.

She held out the red hunting cap to her husband. When he frowned down at it without understanding, she said, "All those guns."

She was equating it with deer season, Marion realized, when it behooved hunters to wear bright colors in the woods so as not to be taken for deer by amateurs who tended to fire at anything that moved. His stomach constricted when it struck him that there might be just as much shooting now, by hunters who relished the thought of open season on Japs.

Mr. Hudkins understood too, then. Accepting the cap, he handed her his felt hat and put on the red one. But even though acceptance of the cap was tacit recognition of danger, he felt called upon to reassure his wife that there wasn't any.

He said, "Now, Helen, nothing's going to come of this. It'll all be over by the time Barney wakes up. Keep the doors and windows locked and stay by the phone."

She nodded. Kissing her on the cheek, he moved past her to open the door.

As Marion started to follow, she suddenly stepped forward and kissed him on the cheek. Marion halted, slightly startled and embarrassed, then gave her a smile of reassurance and followed Mr. Hudkins out the door.

Chapter 22

The Oasis Café was packed.

In one of the booths Captain Bittman sat alone on one side, across from his sergeant driver and the corporal driver of the weapons carrier. The rifles of the noncommissioned officers hung from their shoulders by their slings, the stocks thrusting beneath the table.

The other eleven enlisted men were divided among three booths, four each in two booths and three in the other. Deputy Jake Rollins sat with three posse members in the fifth booth, and four other members of the posse occupied the sixth and last booth. The men were armed with a variety of weapons ranging from deer rifles and carbines to shotguns of various gauges.

The two counters were only partially filled.

At the one parallel to the front door Private Danny Phelps sat by the cash register with a .22 caliber bolt-action Remington rifle propped against the counter next to him. He kept looking toward the booth with only three soldiers in it, as though wondering if he shouldn't be sitting with the others in uniform, but he was too timid to make the first move, and none of those in the booth paid any attention to him.

At the same counter, but with two vacant stools between them, sat the barber with the whiskey-reddened face who had saluted Marion with his raised razor the afternoon Marion hit town. He was armed with a ten-gauge pump shotgun. There was a vacant stool on the other side of the barber, then the last two stools were filled by a couple of posse members with rifles.

The counter facing the service opening which looked

into the kitchen contained only two people. Mr. Elmore and Sheriff Wenzel sat side by side, the former armed with a light 16-guage shotgun, the latter only with his holstered .45.

All of the soldiers, including Captain Bittman, were eating platters of ham and eggs. The captain nervously puffed a cigarette as he ate, alternating bites of food and puffs. The sheriff and a few of the posse members, including the barber, were also eating ham and eggs, but most were only drinking coffee. A number had ordered sandwiches to take along for later, though, and Charlie the cook was busily making those. Rose was moving from booth to booth, pouring coffee.

The puffy-faced barber said to no one in particular, but loudly enough for everyone to hear, "Probably try to kill everyone they can, then commit suicide. Hara-kiri, they call it."

Sheriff Wenzel frowned at him. "They could be miles away by now."

Private Phelps said, "Could be hiding in the weeds right now, waiting for a farm truck."

"Or a school bus," Charlie called from the kitchen with mock ghoulishness.

Savagely slicing at his ham, the barber said, "Goddamn yellow back-stabbing bastards."

The sheriff stopped eating to give him a sharp look. "I think we all ought to simmer down until we find out what's going on," he suggested.

"Simmer down, hell," the barber said roughly. "Those slant-eyes could be raping and killing right this minute."

Private Phelps said in agreement, "God knows what they'd do just to get even with us."

Throwing him an irritated glance, the sheriff returned to his eggs. There was a general silence at both counters, but a murmur of conversation continued to come from the booths.

Danny Phelps looked over at the other soldiers again, this time his attention centering on the booth containing the captain and the two NCO's. At basic training camp he had been terrified of all commissioned officers, but he had formed such a poor opinion of the internment camp commander that he was only mildly afraid of him. The officer companionably eating with two enlisted men both offended Private Phelps's sense of propriety and reflected on the man's wobbly confidence in his authority. While Danny would never dare do it himself, the captain impressed him as the sort of officer an enlisted man could talk back to without being eaten alive. And Private Phelps felt mild contempt for any officer who didn't make him shiver in his boots.

Rose carried a tray of dirty plates behind the counter to set it on the service shelf and picked up several sandwiches bagged to go. Just as she turned, the door opened and her father and Marion came in, both carrying rifles.

Rose momentarily halted to look at Marion with open love. She got a bashful smile in return, bashful because he knew all eyes were on the two of them, and her love was *so* open. Then she moved from behind the counter to deliver the bagged sandwiches.

As Mr. Hudkins and Marion seated themselves at the counter next to Sheriff Wenzel, the attention of everyone in the room centered on Marion. Reactions varied.

Charlie, still building sandwiches just the other side of the service shelf, waved a carving knife in cheery greeting.

Private Phelps thought: *The hero Marine, screw his soul. And the way Rose looked at him!*

The barber was thinking with relish: *Now for some action!*

The sergeant in the booth with the captain was thinking: *Christ, we might as well go back and hit the sack and let this big bastard do it all.*

The captain was feeling relief that at least one professional soldier was present to counterbalance the collection of sad sacks under his command. Maybe he could pick the Marine's brains.

Mr. Elmore was thinking of his dead son Johnny.

Most of the others were merely looking at the uniform and ribbons with admiration and respect.

Sheriff Wenzel, pushing his empty plate aside, said to Mr. Hudkins and Marion, "Guess we can start now. You're the last two." After a pause, he added, "After you've had what you want to eat, of course."

Looking out the front window, Mr. Elmore said, "Blacker than Nick's hatband. Not much point in stumbling around in the dark." Ignoring the Coca-Cola clock on the wall, he took out a gold railroad watch and consulted it. "Forty-two minutes to sun-up."

Rose came back behind the counter and split a smile between her father and Marion.

"Just coffee, darling," her father said.

"Me, too," Marion told her.

As Rose turned toward the urn, Sheriff Wenzel looked over at the captain and said insistently, "Ought to start soon as possible."

The captain's grimace showed his dislike of being the one in charge. After rising to his feet and glancing around at the assemblage, he nervously lit a cigarette from the butt of the one he was smoking. He took a deep puff, exhaled and cleared his throat before finally getting around to saying anything.

When he did speak, in his pronounced Brooklyn accent, it was hardly a demonstration of assured military leadership. He said, "For those who don't know me, I'm Captain Bittman. I got shafted out here, and I don't care who knows it. You know what I do in real life? Children's ready-to-wear, for Chrissake."

He took another deep puff of his cigarette and exhaled. It was apparent from his tone that he regarded his listeners as dumb hicks, and from their expressions that they regarded him as a useless city greenhorn.

"So here's the picture," the captain continued. "Those three tough Japs are from L.A. Just the kind to have zoot suits and switchblades."

Rose set coffee mugs before her father and Marion. Mr. Hudkins was attentively listening to the captain, but neither Rose nor Marion were paying more than perfunctory attention. They were too busy looking at each other.

The barber said, "They got weapons, Captain?"

"M-1's and ammo."

Mr. Hudkins said, "You're positive?"

"Just like my men here," the captain said, gesturing toward the booths full of soldiers. Then he held out both hands, palms up, in a gesture of helplessness. "Wide open for suggestions."

Soldiers looked at each other, and posse members looked at each other, the bald admission from the captain that he didn't know how to handle the situation leaving everyone at a loss. Sheriff Wenzel finally broke the continuing silence by asking, "How'd you find out?"

"Bed check," the captain said promptly. "Then a sentry found the hole in the fence."

Private Phelps asked, "Tracks?" then was unable to keep himself from adding, "Sir?"

Captain Bittman gave him an irritated look. "Dark, soldier."

Mr. Elmore asked quietly, "You aren't issued flashlights?"

The captain said testily, "We weren't about to use lights and get shot."

Mr. Hudkins said, "Then they could have headed anywhere."

Nodding agreement, Captain Bittman said, "And I don't know Rock One about this area."

With a touch of exasperation the sheriff said, "Well, *somebody* has to be in charge."

Deliberately trying to cop out, the captain said, "You're the sheriff."

"With no authority in military matters," the sheriff countered.

Frustrated, searching for somewhere else to pass the buck, the captain's gaze fell on Marion. He said, "I think a Marine'd know something about tactics."

Although only half listening to the debate because his attention was primarily centered on Rose, the comment penetrated Marion's consciousness. Slowly he turned around to look at the captain. He was mildly surprised by the man's flustered expression. Like Danny Phelps, he was conditioned to freeze in the presence of officers, but it was apparent that the captain was somewhat in awe of him.

He would have been less than human not to take advantage of such deliciously reversed roles. Giving the the captain an indulgent smile, he said, "Officers decide tactics, Captain. NCO's only make them work."

There were snickers both from the soldiers and the posse members. The captain's swarthy complexion became even darker.

Mr. Hudkins saved face for the captain by saying, "He's not from here. Knows as little about the land as you do."

Sheriff Wenzel, also trying to pour oil on troubled waters, said, "Look, I'll lend every help I can as a private citizen."

Captain Bittman swung his attention to him. "Well, that's something. So what do we do?"

"I'd get men ten miles each side of town," the sheriff said. "Fan out and work back."

After thinking this over, the captain nodded. "Sounds good. What about you people?"

"We'll work in pairs. Main force toward the river."

Thinking of Mrs. Hudkins and Barney, alone in the house, Marion said, "Sheriff?"

All eyes instantly swung his way. With a touch of shock he realized that everyone there regarded him as the real expert in such matters. He said what he had to say anyway.

"Sheriff, there are women and children in town. I'd put a guard on all four corners of the town, and one on each end of Main Street."

Approving murmurs from all over the room put the tactical suggestion in the same class as a master plan for the invasion of Europe. Rose beamed with pride. Even though he wasn't a real Marine, he was certainly acting like one.

In a tone of relief, Captain Bittman said, "Good deal, Corporal. I'd say that's just about the ballgame."

"Not quite," Mr. Hudkins said quietly. "It's not a ballgame. And it's not a turkey shoot either. We shouldn't have any rounds in the chambers."

Sheriff Wenzel said, "I'll go along with that."

Looking at Mr. Hudkins, the barber said, "Tom, they got guns."

Also looking at Mr. Hudkins, Captain Bittman said peevishly, "I'm a captain in the United States Army, and no civilians tell me what to do."

Forgoing the obvious riposte that only moments before the captain had been doing his best to get the civilian sheriff to take over the whole operation, Mr. Hudkins said equably, "All I'm saying is we shouldn't shoot unless there's no other way."

The barber interceded by saying to Mr. Elmore, "Virgil, I'd guess you'd have something special to say about this."

The attention of all the townspeople in the room centered on Mr. Elmore. The soldiers from the detention camp, including their commanding officer, only looked puzzled, having no way to know that his special interest was having a son die at Pearl Harbor.

Mr. Elmore said heavily, "I understand these young men are American citizens."

"They're *Japs*!" the barber said.

There were murmurs of agreement from the posse members.

In a quiet voice Mr. Elmore said, "I wasn't born in this country."

There was a long period of silence. The barber turned toward Marion for support.

"How about you, Raider?"

All eyes turned to Marion, waiting for his opinion. He said, "They're not soldiers."

"*You*?" the barber said on a high note. "You're wearing the Purple Heart. Shoot you, kill your buddies, and you say *that*?"

"That was there," Marion said. "This is here."

That settled it, insofar as the posse member were concerned. The barber's efforts to inflame the group were scythed down by the simple statement of a boy *who had been there*. Recognizing that any further effort to discredit a hero would turn the whole group against him, the barber discreetly became silent.

Captain Bittman said, "We're moving out now, do it our way. You people want to take chances by going up against 'em without loaded guns, tough shit." Turning toward his men, he said, "Let's move out, men."

The soldiers slid from their booths and trooped out. The captain was last to the door. He paused there to regard Marion with a fishy little smile.

"I thought Marines were tough," he said.

Marion turned slowly to regard the man. In an even voice he said, "Up yours, sir."

The instant he said it, he was appalled. Corporals simply didn't speak to captains that way. The captain was even more appalled, but only because he had no idea of how to handle the situation.

He solved it simply by leaving.

Chapter 23

Marion's bravery had terrified Rose, who expected the captain at the very least to blast him out in front of everyone, at worst to place him under arrest and have him dragged off to the internment camp stockade. When he simply retreated instead, she released her held breath in a sigh of relief. Then she looked at her father in surprise.

Mr. Hudkins, eyes glued tight, was doubled over, strangling with suppressed laughter.

His amusement was infectious. There was a titter from one of the two men seated at the far end of the front counter, another from his companion; it was picked up by someone across the room, then all at once everyone but Danny Phelps and the barber was roaring.

Private Phelps glared at Marion in outrage, seeing nothing funny in disrespect to a superior officer, yet at the same time enviously wishing he had been the one who had made the remark to the captain. The whiskey-faced barber, still smarting from the humiliation of lost face, was at the moment finding nothing funny.

Rose, her momentary terror for Marion now forgotten, fought to keep from breaking up. As the general laughter subsided, she said between snorts of held-back glee, "More coffee?"

Her father gave a weak nod. Marion, red-faced with embarrassment, couldn't even manage a nod. She refilled his cup anyway, then reached over to squeeze his hand.

Sheriff Wenzel turned on his stool to address his deputy, still seated with three posse members in a booth. "Jake, you take care of the guard detail for the town. Pick five men other than yourself and post 'em like the corporal said. One at each corner of the village, one at each end of Main Street."

The aged deputy nodded. "You fellows mind serving as guards?" he asked the three men seated in the booth with him.

When none registered any objection, he picked two more from the booth behind him. Then, rising to his feet, he said, "May as well get in position. Come on, fellows."

The five chosen sentries got up and followed him out. That left only two men in one of the booths, and eight at the counters, including the sheriff.

Glancing around, Sheriff Wenzel said, "We'll work in groups of two, so pick partners."

Mr. Elmore's eyes slid sidewise to settle on Marion. Now recovered from his embarrassment, Marion met his gaze and gave him a slight nod.

Mr. Hudkins had expected Marion to be his partner, but he saw the exchange of glances and graciously yielded, recognizing that it was important to Virgil Elmore to be paired with the Raider corporal. He looked at the barber.

"You need a cool head with you to keep you out of trouble, Bob," he said. "You can go with me."

The barber would have preferred Danny Phelps, whose attitude toward the hunted men was closer to his, but he could hardly offend one of the village's leading citizens. "Sure, Tom," he said glumly.

Danny Phelps was displeased by the choice too, having hoped to be paired with the barber. As it turned out, he got last choice. When the two men in the booth announced that they were partners, and the sheriff picked one of the men at the opposite end of the front counter from Danny, that left only the other man at that end of the counter. He was Harold Colby, the local druggist, a quiet, portly man of middle-age whom Danny regarded as hopelessly square.

Sheriff Wenzel said, "If that captain escapee from Brooklyn does what he's supposed to, he'll have soldiers closing in on the town from all directions. Our job will be to fan outward from this point and hope to catch the escapees in a squeeze between the posse and the soldiers. Virgil, you and the corporal follow the river upstream. Tom, you and Bob check downstream. Harold, you and Danny comb the area north of the river."

He turned to the two men seated in the booth. "You fellows scour the country south. Not much chance they went that way, considering the country, but we have to cover all bets."

The man the sheriff had chosen as a partner asked, "How about us?"

"We'll patrol the main road in both directions, case they're trying to hitchhike out."

The barber emitted a snort. "Figured you'd find a way to work sitting on your butt, Sheriff."

Sheriff Wenzel scowled at him. "Want to switch and come with me, Bob?"

"And miss all chance for a crack at those yellow bastards?" the barber said scornfully. "No thanks."

"Then let's get going. But one last thing. Tom Hudkins had a good point when he said this was no turkey shoot. I want those boys taken alive and unharmed, if at all possible."

Danny Phelps and the barber exchanged glances which meant they didn't accept those instructions as applying to them.

"Any questions?" the sheriff asked.

"No question, but just a reminder," the barber said. "Don't anybody forget these slant-eyes are armed with loaded M-1 rifles. And if you spend too much time waiting for them to drop their guns and throw up their hands, you may catch a slug in the guts while you're waiting."

"I'm not suggesting anyone risk his own life," the sheriff said testily. "I just expect the escapees to be given reasonable chances to surrender. Any other comments?"

When there were none, he rose from his stool. "Let's get moving then."

Everyone else got up too. The sheriff waited for the others to file out before he and his partner followed.

A large number of cars ringed the café. The posse gathered around the sheriff's car, which was parked right in front. Emerging last, the sheriff said, "Everybody knows where he's supposed to be, so let's get to it." He and his partner climbed into the official car, an aisle formed in front of it as men stepped out of the way, and it drove off. The others paired off and began moving on foot toward the street.

Sidling up to Marion, Private Danny Phelps whispered, "Save one for me," then quickly moved away before Marion could reply.

"What did he say?" Mr. Elmore asked with a frown.

"Nothing important, sir," Marion said.

From the café doorway Rose called, "Be careful now, boys."

Mr. Hudkins called back over his shoulder, "Have some coffee up, honey." Then he said to his barber partner in a joking tone but with an undercurrent of seriousness, "Bob, if you shoot and don't have to, I'm going to slit that thick neck with your dull razor."

"Have to catch me first," his partner said.

The two men delegated to search the area south of town turned right at the corner. The other six, walking in pairs a few paces apart, crossed Main Street and took the graveled road past the sheriff's sub-station in the direction of the river.

It was now first light, only minutes before sunrise, still half dark, but light enough to see, and getting lighter by the second.

When they came to the path Marion had twice before taken, they had to go in single file. The sun came up just as they reached the river. It came up gloriously, painting the filmy white clouds lying low on the eastern horizon a mixture of lovely pink and flaming red, and brightly lighting up the whole countryside.

Mr. Hudkins and the barber left them at that point, turning east to work downstream, while the other four continued along the path upstream. At the stepping-stone bridge across the river the four separated into two teams of two each, Private Danny Phelps and the bulky druggist crossing over, Mr. Elmore and Marion leaving the path to continue upstream on this side of the river.

Walking was not difficult, despite there being no path, because the bank was grassy and there was little underbrush. Mr. Elmore, knowing the area, led the way, with Marion following a few paces behind.

They climbed the hill, stopping to rest for a few minutes at the crest. Mr. Elmore moodily surveyed the surrounding countryside. It was not nearly as pretty here atop the plateau as in the valley below. Except for the rushing stream and the Japanese detention camp, there was little to see but the acres of mossy stumps left by the long-ago loggers who had denuded the forest.

Mr. Elmore said, "If they didn't hitchike out, most likely headed north to the county road. That runs into Route Thirteen, and they could hitchhike north on it up into Wyoming and Route Eighty."

"Then you think we're wasting our time up here?" Marion asked.

The railroad man gave a glum nod. "Got to cover it, just in case, though."

He led the way on again.

Back at the Oasis Café Rose helped Charlie scrape the dishes and run them through the dishwasher-sterilizer. Now, with the place tidied up and ready for the morning rush, there was none. Their regular early morning customers were either on guard duty or in the posse. Rose and Charlie sat across from each other in one of the booths of the empty café, sipping coffee. Charlie was also smoking, and a package of cigarettes and a book of matches lay on the table between them.

Rose was terribly nervous about her father and Marion being out in the woods hunting three armed escapees, who for all she knew might be killers. Her hands were shaking so badly that she had to lift the coffee mug with both hands. She kept looking out the window, and when she wasn't doing that, her gaze kept straying to the pack of cigarettes.

Finally she said, "Charlie, those things settle your nerves?"

"Sure," he said. "If you're having a nicotine fit. Course

you wouldn't be having one if you didn't smoke them in the first place."

"Charlie, I want a smoke."

He gave her a pained look. "Oh, Rose, you don't want to start on coffin nails."

"I want one," she said with determination.

Grimacing, he pushed the cigarettes and matches across to her. "Have to light it yourself," he said grumpily.

Putting a cigarette in her mouth, she held flame to it clumsily, her eyes crossing in an effort to focus on the flame, and the match blackening about an inch of cigarette because she held it too far forward. She puffed once, coughed, and her eyes watered. Taking the cigarette from her mouth, she screwed up her nose at it and crushed it out in the ashtray.

Smiling, he said, "Going to write each other?"

After dabbing at her watering eyes with a paper napkin, she nodded. "We promised."

He said in a morose tone, "We're going to cry forty days and forty nights when he takes you away from us."

She smiled at him. "He said this is where he wants to live."

The cook looked pleased at his news. Rose took a sip of her coffee and then stared off into space. After a time her gaze again drifted to the window and she stared worriedly in the direction that Marion and her father and the others had gone.

"Hey!" he said.

She turned to look at him. Deep in her eyes he could see the fear. Reaching across the booth, he patted her hand.

"Don't worry, sweetheart. He's a Marine."

Rose looked as though she were ready to cry. "That's just it," she blurted. "He isn't."

Charlie looked at her without understanding. Now actually crying, she blotted her tears with the paper napkin. He took her other hand in both of his and began patting it.

"Tell old Charlie about it, honey," he said soothingly.

"He never made it through boot camp," Rose said in a

desolate tone. "It wasn't his fault. He just couldn't do the things they wanted him to. Like learn to shoot. He tried, but he just couldn't hit the target. So they threw him out. Not just him, but a whole bunch of others who couldn't make it either. They gave them silly baby blue suits and caps, and travel orders and meal voucher books, and told them to go home and join the Army or Navy."

Bewildered, still methodically patting her hand, he asked, "Where'd he get the Marine uniform?"

"He met this Marine corporal in a Los Angeles bar. The corporal deliberately got him drunk, then rolled him in an alley for his papers and his money and his blue suit. He left his own uniform for Hedge, and two dollars."

Even more bewildered, Charlie asked, "What in the devil for?"

"They were going to send the corporal back overseas. Hedge says he was already an old man at twenty. He deserted."

Releasing her hand, Charlie leaned back in his seat. "My God!"

Rose's tears had now stopped flowing as she became intent on making the cook understand that none of the fault had been Marion's. "Hedge didn't want to report the man and have him arrested for desertion, because he felt sorry for him. And he couldn't walk out of the alley in his underwear. So he just put on the uniform and started hitchhiking home."

After taking a thoughtful sip of coffee, Charlie frowned off into space. After a time, he said, "Really not much else he could do that I can see."

"I knew you'd understand," she said mistily, reaching across to give his hand a squeeze. "But will you do me a favor?"

"Sure, honey. Name it."

"Don't tell Dad or Mr. Elmore. I'm sure Dad could take it, but he might tell Barney, and he probably couldn't. And it would kill Mr. Elmore."

Charlie gave her a reassuring smile. "Don't worry, Rose. Compared to me, clams babble."

Chapter 24

Danny Phelps was becoming less and less happy with the man he had drawn as a partner. The overweight druggist was slowing him down. He not only was unable to move as fast as the Army private would have liked, he had to stop to rest every few minutes. On top of that, he kept arguing with Danny about the route.

Danny had been steering them in the general direction of the county road, having come to the same general conclusion Mr. Elmore had that the three Japanese escapees would probably head for it and follow it until it hit Route 13, then take it north. Harold Colby had no objection to that, as long as it was the easiest route. But whenever the going got a little rough, the druggist argued for a change in direction along some easier route.

About a mile beyond the river they ran into a path leading in the right direction, but after a couple of hundred yards the path veered off to the northeast. Danny wanted to continue on due north, but Harold Colby wanted to stay on the path.

"There's nothing off that way," the Army private told him. "It's a game path that just goes deep into the woods."

"Those Japs wouldn't know that," Colby argued. "They don't know this area. Logical thing would be for them to follow the path."

"If they ever looked at a map, they'd never take that path," Danny said in exasperation. "And you can bank on it they somehow got hold of a map. Hell, every filling station has them, and they been around here a couple of years. They'll know where they're going, because while the little bastards may be sneaky, they sure ain't dumb."

He gestured in a northerly direction. "Let's go this way. I'm Army, see, so I don't have to take orders from civilians."

The plump druggist didn't like it, but he gave in because he really knew very little about the countryside. He was not a hunter, and this was the first time he had ever been north of the river on foot. Reluctantly he followed the uniformed boy.

About a half mile farther on, they came to the crest of a small rise that looked down into a narrow valley no more than two hundred yards across. On the opposite side of the valley brush-covered slopes climbed upward again. They paused under the cover of the drooping branches of a weeping willow to study the area ahead.

When he saw a movement in the brush on the opposite slope, Danny made an urgent movement and sank to one knee. Sinking to one knee also, the druggist peered that way, his fingers on the bolt of his rifle, ready to throw a shell into the chamber if it turned out that the escapees were over there.

Two figures pushed from between the bushes on the opposite slope. But they weren't Japanese. They were uniformed and helmeted soldiers.

"Jesus Christ!" Danny said disgustedly. "The pincher's closed, and the little yellow bastards aren't in it."

Coming to his feet again, he moodily regarded the two soldiers descending the slope across the valley. Harold Colby also climbed to his feet.

"Well, they didn't come this way," Danny said to his partner. "May as well head back."

"Shouldn't we wait for those soldiers to join us?" the druggist asked.

"You wait for them if you want," Danny said irritably. "I'm heading back for where the action is."

That was probably wherever that big Marine corporal was, he thought. He should have shaken this fat slob long ago in order to cut back and trail the Raider. The Marine not only knew all the wiles of jungle fighting, he probably knew how Japs thought, and had figured out exactly where the three would be hiding out.

Suddenly sick at the thought of the Marine Raider getting all the glory while he played nursemaid to a wheezing fat man, Private Phelps abruptly headed back toward the river. Frowning after him, the druggist considered calling to him to wait, then decided the hell with it and shrugged. Turning to look toward the soldiers again, he saw they were now nearly to the bottom of the slope. He pushed through the drooping branches of the weeping willow tree, waved to them and called, "Hallo!"

Both men halted, stared over at him, then waved back and started to pick their way across the valley.

Meantime Marion and Mr. Elmore were still working their way upstream. About a half mile beyond the Japanese detention camp they came to a spot where the stream both widened and deepened to form a pool. Someone had built a diving board on the near bank. Young trees lined the grassy banks on both sides, screening out the depressing view of the ravaged land.

Stopping next to the diving board, Mr. Elmore looked out across the pool from saddened eyes.

"We used to come out here all the time," he said.

He meant with his dead son, Marion realized, feeling sorrow for the man.

Mr. Elmore took out his gold railroad watch and looked at it. "Six-forty-five," he said. Then he gave Marion an inquiring look. "You own a watch?"

"No, sir," Marion said.

At the end of the gold chain attached to the watch there was a ring clipped to one of Mr. Elmore's belt loops. Unclipping it, he held the watch and chain out to Marion.

In a formal tone he said, "You'll discover when you take off the back, it can be adjusted to the climate you find yourself in."

Looking at the watch, but making no move to take it, Marion said, "Please, I can't accept this."

Mr. Elmore continued to hold it out. Swallowing, Marion shook his head.

"It's important to me," the railroad man said quietly.

The look in his eyes made it impossible for Marion to refuse. Reluctantly he took the watch, lifted the right front corner of his jacket to drop it into his watch pocket, and clipped the chain to a belt loop in such a way that it wouldn't hang below the bottom edge of the jacket.

He said humbly, "I hope I can deserve it, sir."

Looking at his ribbons, Mr. Elmore said, "You already deserve it."

That succeeded in making Marion feel terrible. There was no way he could give back the gift, though. He simply had to suffer his guilt.

Mr. Elmore was gazing out across the pool again. Finally he sighed, began to move on, then halted and turned.

"That Phelps boy. What did he say to you back there?"

Considering, Marion decided there was no reason the man shouldn't know. "To save him one."

Mr. Elmore's face turned to stone. "He and Colby are the ones going to find them, if they're found."

His expression made Marion feel uncomfortable. He began to wish he had told Mr. Elmore of the remark when he first asked about it.

Mr. Elmore said flatly, "He plans to shoot them on sight."

"Won't the fellow with him prevent that?" Marion ventured.

Mr. Elmore's tone wasn't exactly scornful, but it hardly indicated great confidence in the druggist. "No," he said simply. He gestured upstream. "You can cover this alone. I'm going after that boy and take away his gun. I just hope to God I'm in time."

Before Marion could frame any answer, he hurried off downstream. Marion gazed after him until he was out of sight, then shrugged and went over to sit on the diving board.

After a time he got up and moved upstream again. But when he emerged from the clump of trees surrounding the pool and got a good view of the country ahead, he halted in discouragement. The view was unobstructed for more than a mile, and there was nothing to see except the stream winding past thousands of tree stumps.

There were no Japanese hiding there, he was sure. Mr. Elmore had virtually admitted it was a waste of time to search for them in this direction anyway. He decided to turn around and go back.

Far downstream, a couple of miles below the stepping-stone bridge, Tom Hudkins and his barber partner were coming to a similar conclusion. They had reached a point at the western edge of the valley where the stream entered a narrow canyon between low hills. The banks were too steep for them to continue alongside the stream. They were either going to have to climb over the hill at a point some distance from the stream, or turn back.

Gazing up at the hill, the barber said in a sullen voice, "I don't think they came this way."

"Frankly, neither do I," Tom Hudkins said. "My guess is they headed north to the county road, in the area Harold Colby and young Phelps are covering."

Without further conversation they started back.

Private Danny Phelps was within about fifty yards of the stepping-stone bridge when he spotted moving bushes on the other side of the river. Fading behind a tree, he dropped prone and levered a shell into the chamber of his .22 rifle.

His sights were trained on the point he figured whoever was causing the bushes to move would emerge from the underbrush. But his finger on the trigger relaxed when he saw Mr. Elmore step forth.

He was about to climb to his feet and call to the brakeman, but the man's grim expression changed his mind. He watched him gingerly make the crossing, almost losing his balance when he slipped on one of the spray-covered stones in the center of the stream, but finally jumping safely to the other side. Danny lay quietly where he was as Mr. Elmore passed within ten yards of his hiding place and continued on north.

Where was the man going, he wondered?

Then it hit him. With a surge of excitement he decided that Mr. Elmore would never have left the Marine corporal unless he had been sent. And the only thing the corporal could have sent him for was reinforcements. That meant they must have spotted the three Japs without the Japs spotting them. The big Raider must be keeping them under observation while Mr. Elmore went after more fire power.

But why would a battle-wise Raider need reinforcements against a mere three Japs? More likely the glory-hungry bastard had pretended he needed help in order to get Mr. Elmore out of the way, so that he could pick off all three of the Japs by himself.

As soon as Mr. Elmore was out of sight, Danny jumped to his feet and ran the remaining distance to the stepping-stones. He went across quickly, skipping from rock to rock much more gracefully than the older man had. On the other side he began to lope upstream.

About three-quarters of the way up the rise toward the plateau, Danny heard a stick crack from somewhere beyond the crest of the rise. It sounded to him as though it had cracked under someone's heavy foot. Instantly he faded into some tall grass a dozen yards from the bank and dropped flat.

The big Marine corporal came over the crest and started down, moving at a leisurely pace, his rifle held at trail position. While his gaze seemed to be taking in the surroundings on both sides of the stream, he didn't seem to be exercising any particular caution.

The man wasn't behaving at all as though he thought any Japs might be lurking in the bushes. Which would be normal behavior for a trained jungle fighter only if he *knew* there was no danger.

He had already killed them, Danny thought sickly. He had grabbed off all the glory for himself. No shots had sounded, but that meant nothing. Those damned Raiders were rumored to carry garroting wires, and they had been trained to move in behind Japs like ghosts.

When the Marine had passed by, Danny came to his feet and began to follow. Maybe he had missed out on the fun, he thought, but at least he could get a little perverse satisfaction from trailing the jungle expert without the big jerk being aware of it.

He kept well back, about a hundred yards, to make absolutely sure he wouldn't be detected. He therefore was not a witness to the drama at the stepping-stone crossing until it had been underway for some time.

Chapter 25

Thin Tommy Masamura was the first of the trio to wake up. Climbing from the pile of dried leaves that had served as a blanket through the chilly night, he shivered in his thin denim pants and jacket. Although the sun was well up and was shining from a clear sky, sunshine didn't penetrate through the screening branches of the weeping willow beneath which the boys had spent the night. It looked as though it was warm outdoors, but it was still quite cool under there.

Tommy looked at the still sleeping Joe Harukawa and Jimmy Katsu, both buried to their necks in dead leaves, then he peered through the shielding weeping willow branches at the barbwire encampment only fifty yards away. As he watched, a bugle sounded Mess Call, and a mixture of soldiers, Japanese women, men, and children began to emerge from the tin-roofed huts to converge on the mess hall.

They had slept right through both Reveille and Assembly, Tommy thought. He had better awaken the others.

He did it by placing the tip of his center finger against the ball of his thumb, then snapping it against their noses. Both sat up abruptly. Plump Joe Harukawa gave Tommy an aggrieved look. The powerfully muscled Jimmy Katsu said threateningly, "I ought to whomp your ass, you slant-eyed sonovabitch."

Unperturbed by the threat, Tommy said, "Time to get up, slopeheads. Mess Call just blew."

Climbing to his feet and brushing leaves from himself, Joe peered through the drooping branches at the compound. "What good's that do us?" he inquired.

"It told us the time," Jimmy said sourly, also climbing to his feet. "Seven-thirty."

Still peering toward the compound, plump Joe Harukawa said in a worried voice, "Captain Bittman's jeep isn't parked in front of headquarters." He glanced around at Tommy. "Thought you said that by morning they'd figure we were long gone from around here, and would give up looking."

"How you know he's still looking?" Tommy inquired. "Maybe he's off chasing some dame."

"At chow time?" Joe said. "Don't be silly. The Brooklyn chow hound miss a meal?"

Squat Jimmy Katsu, also gazing toward the compound, said, "That weapons carrier isn't in the motor pool either. Those bastards are still out looking for us." He swung an accusing gaze at Tommy. "You said if we holed up here, where they'd never dream checking so close by, we could walk out free as birds by morning."

"We probably can," Tommy said in a defensive tone. "They have to figure we made it to the county road and on up into Wyoming. Bittman must have turned it over to the Feds by now. There shouldn't be roadblocks any nearer than fifty or a hundred miles."

"Then where's Bittman and that sad-sack search detail we watched him lead out last night?" Jimmy asked.

Tommy, after peering toward the barbwire enclosure again, said with a touch of uncertainty, "Just to make sure, we could stick it out here till tonight, I guess. They'd be bound to give up by then."

"And eat what?" Joe demanded.

Jimmy growled, "You could live a week on your fat."

"You could do the same on the fat in your head," the plump boy shot at him.

"I haven't got any either place," Tommy said, rubbing his lean tummy. "I'm getting hungry."

Joe said, "Maybe we could crawl back through the hole in the fence, grab chow and take off again. Our people wouldn't give us away, and we all look alike to those fart-head guards."

Jimmy said, "You can see from here they patched up

the hole." He looked at Tommy. "Okay, mastermind, what's our move now?"

"What's wrong with our original plan?" Tommy countered.

"The search detail isn't back."

"That doesn't mean they're still looking for us around here," Tommy said. "Maybe they all stumbled over their own feet, fell in the river and drowned. You've watched 'em march, haven't you?"

Joe said, "I don't know what you guys are going to do, but I'm going to find some breakfast."

"Where?" Jimmy inquired.

The plump boy shrugged. "Swipe some eggs from a farmer's chicken coop, maybe. Or find a real isolated farmhouse and terrorize 'em into feeding us. Give 'em the old Fu Manchu look."

"He was Chinese, not Japanese, noggin-head," Tommy told him. "More likely we'd end up with our asses full of buckshot anyway."

"Well, I'm not going to sit here all day," Joe said. "You guys want to, I'll take off alone."

"I thought it was one-for-all and all-for-one," muscular Jimmy Katsu said.

"Okay," Tommy said, "I better lead the way, so you two stumblebums don't fall in the river."

After peering once more in the direction of the internment camp, he dropped to all fours and began crawling toward the edge of the plateau, carefully keeping the weeping willow tree between himself and the compound. The other two dropped to their hands and knees and crawled after him.

When they had crawled over the rim and far enough down the slope so that their heads wouldn't show above it, they rose to their feet and made their precarious way along the slope to the path running alongside the stream. It was touchy going, because the ground inclined downward at such a steep pitch that they had to cling to bits of underbrush to steady themselves as they moved along. They all made it to the path, however, without anyone losing his balance and sliding down the hill on the seat of his pants.

They started downward on the path.

A half mile north of the river Virgil Elmore heard voices coming from a short distance ahead. He discreetly faded behind a tree until he could determine whether the conversationalists were posse members or the Japanese escapees.

A moment later he recognized the voice of Harold Colby and stepped out from behind the tree again. The druggist was saying, "Think that stepping-stone bridge is this way, but I'm no woodsman."

A helmeted soldier carrying a rifle appeared from the underbrush a dozen yards away, followed by the overweight druggist, who in turn was followed by a second soldier. They all momentarily halted when they spotted the railroad man standing there, then moved on to stop again in a semicircle around him.

"Virgil," the druggist said. "What are you doing out here?"

"Where's the Phelps boy?" Elmore asked.

"Took off. Said something about heading back for where the action was."

Elmore frowned. "Meaning what?"

Harold Colby shrugged. "When we spotted the soldiers here, closing in from the other direction, we knew the Japs weren't out this way. I guess what he meant was he figured they were still holed up around the river somewhere."

Whirling, the railroad man strode off in the direction from which he had just come. The soldiers and Colby gazed after him until he disappeared from sight, then looked at each other and shrugged. They continued on at a leisurely pace.

About that time Marion was just reaching the bottom of the hill on the opposite side of the stream. He continued along the bank to where the rapids gurgled around and over the many boulders strewn in the stream bed at that point. When he came to the stepping-stone bridge, he hunkered down in a squatting position, his rifle across his knees, to enjoy the beauty of the scene.

His gaze drifted across the field of yellow flowers on the opposite bank to the spot where he had seen the drinking woodchuck, then moved on to the place where he and Rose had made love among the flowers. He had totally forgotten to pick her any flowers afterward, it suddenly occurred to him, and that had been their ostensible reason for coming here in the first place.

A movement on the other side of the stream, off to his left, intruded on the corner of his vision. He glanced that way just in time to see three Japanese youths coming along the path in single file. They were the same three he had seen inside the barbwire enclosure, backs to the flag, arms defiantly folded, when Retreat was blowing. They were all rather short, perhaps five feet eight inches, all wore their hair ducktail style, and they were all dressed in denim pants, denim jackets and heavy work shoes. The leader was lean-waisted and slim, the second one slightly plump, and the third had the squat, powerful body of a wrestler.

In his hunkered-down stance the Japanese didn't see Marion. But they did when he suddenly rose to his feet. Coming to sudden halts, they stared across the roaring water at him and at his cradled rifle. When he swung the rifle muzzle in their general direction, their eyes became fearful. The fear increased when he worked the bolt of the rifle.

There was enough hate mixed with the fear to give them bravery, though. The thin youth in the lead shouted above the roar of the rapids, "Go ahead and shoot, you Marine sonovabitch!"

"Yeah!" the squat, heavy-muscled youth called. "Get yourself another gook! That's what you call us, isn't it?"

Marion, surprised at himself for acting so much like a real Marine, called back calmly, "Just give up your guns and cross on over."

"Guns?" the thin one said. "Who the hell's got guns?"

Frowning, Marion called, "The captain said you had."

"Captain Bittman, the Brooklyn moron?" the thin boy sneered.

The burly one shouted, "Shove it, hero."

The plump boy in the middle, who had so far not said a word, looked more frightened than the other two. Lowering his rifle muzzle, Marion appealed to him. "I'm no hero. I'm not even a Marine. But I'm tired of talking. Get on over here."

The words had no effect, except to make the plump boy look even more frightened. He made no more effort to obey than the other two. Marion elevated the muzzle to cover them again. Still they made no move.

"I said get over!" Marion said harshly, beginning to become irritated.

"Why?" the burly boy asked just as harshly. "So they can relocate us in Cincinnati? What do we do there? Who do we talk to?"

The thin boy said, "All we know's the Cincinnati Reds."

The plump youth suddenly found his voice. He shouted, "It's L.A. or nothing, man. Born there."

It was a stalemate. They were daring him to shoot, and he couldn't. He decided to try reason.

"It's either come over or get your butts shot off by some trigger-happy soldier!" he called.

They frowned at this, then looked at each other. Marion called, "I'm not the only one. Woods full of men who just might shoot. Fact one soldier intends to, on sight."

That jarred them. They held rapid converse in Japanese, then the thin youth called above the sound of the water, "That uniform. Battle ribbons."

"Forget 'em," Marion said dismissingly. "Just get on over here."

They made no move.

"What you going to do?" Marion asked disgustedly. "Walk to Los Angeles?"

Again they conversed in Japanese. When they looked back at him, the faces of all three registered defeat.

The thin boy said, "No hands-up talk. Coming over like men."

"It's okay by me," Marion said, relieved. "Just come on over."

The thin youth stepped out onto the boulder nearest the bank. He stood there for some moments, dubiously studying the precarious route, before venturing onto the next. Before each step he studied the boulder he was going to step onto carefully. When he reached the first of the center rocks that were constantly covered by spray, he slipped slightly, recovered his balance and looked terrified.

"Easy now," Marion said. "That's good."

"Shit it is," the Japanese told him. "I can't swim."

Chapter 26

Eventually the thin Japanese screwed up sufficient courage to jump to the next boulder. This one too was wet with spray, and his feet slipped again. He did a terrified little jig to regain his balance, and when he finally managed to regain it, he froze. Marion could tell by his glazed eyes that he wasn't going to move from that spot, at least for the time being.

From the bank behind him the burly Japanese called encouragingly, "You got it now, Tommy."

Rigid, staring down at the rushing water, the thin boy said, "Your ass I got it."

The plump boy said, "Water's not that deep."

"Well, why don't you jump in and show me!" the boy stranded in midstream snarled.

Marion realized what he had to do. He stepped from the bank onto the first boulder on his side.

"Hold it," he said. "I'll come out and help you."

The squat, thick-muscled escapee called mockingly, "That's right, Tommy. Marine coming to save you."

The plump youth called, "Hey, man, got a match?"

The stranded boy spat out, *"Shi zu-ka ni-shiro dareka ku-ru."*

In pretended shock the squat Japanese said, "Know what he said, Marine? He said, 'Shut up, you crazy bastards.' May be his last words too, before he drowns."

Marion stopped on the boulder which left only one other boulder between them. He said, "Hold on now," and considered what he was going to do next. If he stepped onto the next boulder, he would be close enough to hold out a hand to the stranded youth, but there wasn't room on the next boulder for both of them.

The squat escapee said, "Speak English, man."

The plump one said, "Yeah, Marine. Don't help him unless he says please in English."

The thin youth gazed down at the spray soaking his feet in an agony of terror. He yelled, *"Jo dung wa vo se!"*

"There he goes again," the burly Japanese said, howling with laughter. "He said he'll break our necks."

Marion found himself having to repress a grin. The marooned boy was really in danger of nothing worse than a thorough wetting, because the water wasn't deep enough to drown him. And his two friends were having the times of their lives needling him.

He said admonishingly, but also with amusement, "You guys shut up. Not helping a bit."

The burly youth stepped from the bank onto the first boulder, then easily skipped across others to halt on the one immediately behind the stranded boy. He said, "Hey, watch, Marine. When I goose him, he'll go right over the trees."

The thin boy yelled, *"Yo tarra koro su zo!"*

Both his friends reacted with mock horror. The plump one, still on land, said, "Such language!" The one immediately behind him said to Marion, "Touch him and he'll kill me, he said. And called me a piece of shit. Can you believe a nice, well-mannered Japanese boy would talk like that?"

"You guys are nuts," Marion said. "Shut up while I figure this out."

The solution occurred to him then. Grasping the rifle by the end of its stock, he held the muzzle out across the rock between them. "Here, grab it."

Staring into the muzzle, the thin boy returned to English. "Jesus, not *that* way!"

Marion pulled the rifle back, grabbed it by the barrel and started to hold out the stock. "Careful," he said. "It's got a round in the chamber."

Looking at the stock, but not reaching for it, the stranded boy said, "Well, put the safety on."

Drawing back the rifle a second time, Marion examined it. He looked at both sides, its top, turned it over and studied its underside. Finally looking up, he said, "Can't find it."

"You're no Marine, all right," the thin boy said disgustedly.

"Not my rifle." He fumbled with it some more. "Where *is* it?"

The plump boy said, "Shit, we'll be here till the war's over."

He started to laugh. The heavily muscled youth, still on the boulder behind his thin friend, started to laugh too. The thin boy joined in. Marion looked up, tried to hold his face straight, gave up and began to giggle.

The three Japanese managed to control their laughter after a time. Tears in his eyes, the thin boy gazed at Marion in wonder and said, "Man, I don't believe you."

Marion managed to control his giggling also. Still unable to find the safety, he thought of another solution.

"I'll just clean it out," he said, and started working the bolt to eject the shells into the water.

Staring past his thin friend at Marion with a disbelieving expression on his face, the burly Japanese said, "Terrific!"

The plump youth, just as unbelieving, said, "A genius!"

Marion continued snapping the bolt until the gun was empty. Again he offered it muzzle-first to the stranded boy. The youth eyed it with apprehension.

"You sure?" he asked doubtfully, making no move to reach for it.

With an exasperated sigh, Marion withdrew it, aimed the gun at the water and pulled the trigger. There was a click. The Japanese youth was still apprehensive, though.

"Could be a misfire," he said.

The boy behind him said, "Yeah, white man speak with forked tongue."

That set all four of them laughing again.

Marion recovered first. "Cut it out, you guys," he said. He started to hold out the rifle muzzle again, then said, "Oh, hell," reversed it and held out the stock.

The thin youth grabbed the stock, Marion pulled on the muzzle, and the Japanese jumped onto the next boulder. Although that boulder was dry, the soles of his feet were soaking wet, and he started to slip for the third time. There was a minor tug-of-war, with the Japanese pulling on the rifle stock in a terrified attempt to keep himself from falling backward, and Marion pulling on the muzzle.

At that moment Private Danny Phelps arrived at the bottom of the hill. For an instant he stood frozen at sight of the Marine Raider and a Japanese struggling over a rifle in midstream. Then he dropped to one knee and sighted the .22 at the thin Japanese. The big jungle-fighter hero had gotten himself in trouble, he exulted, and Private Danny Phelps was coming to the rescue.

He squeezed the trigger.

Marion heard the sharp crack of a small-caliber rifle from somewhere behind him. At the same moment he felt a blow beneath his right shoulder blade, as though someone had punched him in the back. Although there was no particular pain, dizziness instantly washed over him.

Releasing his grip on the rifle muzzle, he toppled into the water. The thin Japanese had just managed to recover his balance, but his grip on the rifle stock was at its very end, and when Marion released the other end, gravity jerked loose his grip. The weapon tumbled into the water also.

Private Phelps, horrified by his mistake, was nevertheless still full of battle fervor. He swung his rifle sights to center on the muscular Japanese just behind the one who had dropped the rifle. When he realized the man was unarmed, he checked his trigger squeeze and swung the sights again, to center on the third escapee standing on the opposite bank.

Again checking his trigger squeeze just in time, when he realized that none of them were armed, he jumped to his feet and ran forward.

The thin Japanese in midstream shouted at him furiously, "You stupid bastard dogface!"

Then the man jumped into the water, which came only to his waist, and began floundering toward where Marion was clinging to a boulder he had slammed against ten yards downstream. The other two Japanese jumped into the water also and began wading that way.

Dropping his rifle, Danny Phelps ran along the bank until he was opposite Marion and plunged in too.

Fifty yards downstream Tom Hudkins and his partner heard the shot and began running toward the sound. Fifty yards north of the river Virgil Elmore heard it also, recognized it as the sound of a .22, and raced toward the stepping-stone bridge. Fifty yards behind him druggist Harold Colby and the two soldiers heard it and began to run that way. Just turning off on the path leading toward the river from the graveled street at the edge of town, Sheriff Wenzel and his partner heard it and began to run also.

Dazed, Marion's grip on the boulder began to fail. He could see the Army private and the three Japanese floundering through the water toward him, but he could also see his blood coloring the foaming water. The latter sight made the strength flow from his arms; he lost his grip and was buffeted downstream.

Mr. Elmore reached the bridge, took in the situation at a glance, and began to race downstream along the north bank. Danny Phelps, sputtering from boulder to boulder, looked up at him pleadingly as he ran by and gasped, "Aimed at the Jap—thought they were fighting."

Except that his face tightened, there was no reaction from the running man.

Marion had come to rest with his back against another boulder. Blood now dribbled from a corner of his mouth, and his blank expression indicated he was going into shock. Dropping his 16-gauge shotgun, Mr. Elmore jumped into the water and began wading toward him.

Farther upstream Danny Phelps and the three Japanese were still flailing their way downstream, the thin Japanese, terrified at stepping into a hole that would take him over his head, making the slowest progress because he kept making panic-stricken grabs at boulders. Clinging to one boulder, he shouted, "Hang on, Marine!"

Just as Mr. Elmore reached for him, Marion was washed from the boulder his back rested against and began to tumble downstream.

Tom Hudkins and his partner appeared on the south bank. Running along the path right behind them appeared Sheriff Wenzel and his partner. Pointing at Marion, being tumbled over and over downstream, Mr. Elmore shouted, "He's been shot by the Phelps boy!"

Mr. Hudkins and the barber, neither of whom could swim, stood gaping helplessly. Coming to a panting halt, the sheriff snapped at the barber, "Get my car. Parked on the Oasis lot."

The barber began to lumber up the path in the direction of the town, his heavy shotgun held at high port.

Marion came to rest with his leg caught between two boulders. His eyes rolled up in his head and his face sank below the surface. The foaming water above his face turned pink.

"Somebody grab him!" Tom Hudkins called frantically.

The squat, powerfully built Japanese, too far upstream to reach Marion in time, yelled with equal franticness, "Going to drown!"

The thin Japanese, even farther upstream, shouted, "Jesus, SAVE HIM!"

Private Phelps abandoned wading and began to breaststroke downstream. The two Japanese tried swimming with clumsy overhand strokes, but gave it up when they both crashed into boulders and resumed merely wading again.

Harold Colby and the two soldiers appeared on the north bank. All three dropped their rifles, the soldiers threw aside their helmets, and they all jumped into the stream.

Marion's face came above the water, he gasped once, then it sank below the surface again. Would-be-rescuers floundered toward him from all directions.

It was Virgil Elmore who reached him first. Bracing against the current, the railroad man gripped Marion's jacket front with his right hand, put his left behind his head, and forced his face above water. The wounded youth was unconscious and blood flowed from a corner of his mouth in a steady trickle.

Then the heavy-muscled Japanese got there. Encircling Mr. Elmore's waist with both arms, he braced a foot against one of the boulders and pushed backward against the current. Slowly Mr. Elmore backed up, pulling Marion erect. They all backed farther, until Marion's caught foot pulled free of the cleft between the two boulders.

Then the plump Japanese boy, Danny Phelps, Harold Colby and the two soldiers all got there at once. A human chain was formed to work the wounded boy over to the bank. He was pulled up and laid on his back on the grass.

Chapter 27

The rescuers stood panting and dripping water. Kneeling next to Marion, Mr. Hudkins on one side and Sheriff Wenzel on the other stripped off his jacket, necktie and shirt. When they had difficulty getting off his undershirt, Mr. Elmore reached between them, gripped it at the throat and ripped it down the center.

The sheriff's partner, who had not been in the water, said, "Bleeding at the mouth. Lung shot. Get him warm." Stripping off the hunting jacket he was wearing, he held it out. No one paid any attention to him. Mr. Hudkins rolled the wounded boy over on his stomach.

Without much conviction Sheriff Wenzel said, "He'll make it. Strong kid."

Harold Colby, still panting long after everyone else had regained breath, said between pants, "Near drowned. How'd it happen?"

Danny Phelps said miserably, "I thought they were fighting. They were out in the middle, Hedge and that one there." He nodded toward the thinnest Japanese. "I didn't know Hedge was holding out his rifle to help him across. It looked like—"

His pathetic plea faded under Mr. Elmore's uncompromising gaze.

Mr. Hudkins ripped the skivvy shirt the rest of the way off and used it to wipe away the blood welling from the bullet hole.

The man who had offered the jacket said, "Lung, all right. Stick a rag or something in there."

"Strong-looking blood," the sheriff commented hopefully.

He got up from his kneeling position, and Mr. Elmore knelt next to Marion in his place. The railroad man forced the tip of his little finger into the bullet hole. "Something dry on him," he said.

The sheriff's partner eagerly offerred his hunting jacket again. Mr. Hudkins this time accepted it, draping it across Marion's back, and incidentally over Mr. Elmore's forearm.

Sheriff Wenzel said, "Where's that goddamned barber I sent after my car?"

Fat Harold Colby, now with his breath recovered, said reasonably, "Couldn't drive it down here, Sheriff. I'll go check."

He waddled off up the path.

Mr. Elmore, his hand beneath the jacket, muttered, "Dang war. Dang war."

Mr. Hudkins said, "Have to carry him to the car." His tone became brisk. "All right. Head, feet, some at the middle."

The burly Japanese and the plump one each took a leg, gripping it at the knee and the ankle. The two soldiers each supported a shoulder. Danny Phelps knelt to slide his hands beneath the wounded boy's stomach. Mr. Elmore, on the other side, shoved his left hand beneath Marion's middle without removing his right little finger from the bullet hole. Mr. Hudkins took hold of Marion's head.

"Okay, up," he said.

Everyone straightened, lifting Marion from the ground still in a face-down position. With the sheriff leading the way, they carried him along the path. The sheriff's partner and the third Japanese brought up the rear. They met the fat druggist coming back, where the path turned toward town.

"Bob parked where the path comes out," he told the sheriff. "Just been waiting there." Nodding, the sheriff shooed him back the way he had come.

When they carried the wounded youth out onto the graveled road, the barber got out from behind the wheel of the sheriff's car and opened the rear door. But before

Marion could be loaded into the back seat, Rose came hurrying along the street in her waitress uniform.

With the hunting jacket covering the upper part of his body, and with the men supporting his body obstructing her view, she did not immediately recognize that it was Marion being supported.

"Dad, what is it?" she asked worriedly. "I saw Bob drive off fast in the sheriff's car, and figured—" She let it trail off, her gaze suddenly darting around in search of Marion.

"Accidental shooting," her father said. "We have to get him over to the hospital at Riverton."

She moved closer to peer at the victim, and her expression became stricken. Kneeling, she looked into his down-turned face.

"Hedge?" she said beseechingly.

His eyes opened, but looked straight through her. Blood oozed from his mouth. Then his eyes focused and recognition appeared in them. His lips moved, and very faintly he said, "Rose."

"Yes?" she whispered.

"Not going to die."

"No," she said with a mixture of despair and pleading.

"Tell about me."

"It doesn't matter," she said, tears beginning to run down her cheeks.

"Matters to me," he said, barely audibly. "Promise?"

"Promise," she agreed in a breaking voice.

His eyes went vacant again. She rose to her feet, and they carried him on to the car.

When Marion awakened, he was in a hospital bed. He felt weak, and there was a pain in the right side of his chest. His head felt entirely clear, though. He couldn't move his left arm, because it was strapped down. When he looked up, he saw why. A bottle of blood and another bottle of clear fluid hung from a rack next to the bed, with tubes running from them to his arm.

He glanced around the room. There was another bed next to his, but it was empty. Looking down toward the foot of his own bed, he spotted a call button safety-pinned to the sheet near his right hand. He pressed the button.

Almost immediately a middle-aged nurse came hurrying into the room. When she saw him awake, she smiled hugely. "Decided to rejoin us, have you?" she said.

"Where am I?" he asked, surprised at the weakness of his voice.

"Riverton General Hospital. To anticipate your next question, it's Tuesday."

"I've been out for twenty-four hours?"

"More like thirty-two or three," she said. "It's four-thirty P.M. Tuesday. They got the bullet out of your lung, the doctor says it isn't badly damaged, and your pulse has been strong. We think you'll survive."

"Can I see anyone?" he asked.

"That's up to the doctor. I'll go tell him you're awake."

She popped a thermometer into his mouth and left the room. When she returned a few minutes later, she removed the thermometer, read it and entered his temperature on a chart attached to the foot of his bed.

"Well?" he asked.

"Couple of degrees," she said. "But that's normal with a bullet hole in your lung."

"I mean visitors."

"Oh. Dr. Manning will be along in a minute."

Dr. Manning turned out to be a lean, elderly man with a full head of white hair. After taking Marion's pulse and listening to his chest with a stethoscope, he grunted and said, "Only way to kill you, young fellow, would be cut off your head and bury it ten feet from your body."

"How long will I be laid up, sir?" Marion asked.

"Couple of months before you can turn somersaults. But only a couple of weeks before you'll be up and about."

"Can I have visitors?"

"Don't see why not, long as you don't overtire yourself. Hungry?"

Thinking about it, Marion realized he was. "Haven't eaten since Sunday night," he said.

"Sure you have." The doctor pointed toward the bottle

of clear fluid. "Intravenously. Hardly comes up to meat and potatoes, though. I'll chart you for regular diet."

Marion's hunger increased. "When's chow?" he asked.

"Believe the kitchen aides start bringing dinner about five." He glanced at a watch. "Quarter to now." He looked at the blood bottle, now nearly empty. "Barring complications, won't need any more blood. I'll have the nurse disconnect you from both of these."

After he left, the nurse came in and freed him of the arm tubes. She cranked up his bed so that he was in a seated position before she left again. Only minutes after that a dietician's aide wheeled a food cart to the door, set a bed tray in front of him and served him a meal.

Visiting hours were from seven to nine. Promptly at seven Rose entered the room. Her eyes became radiant when she saw him sitting up in bed. She bent to kiss him, then sat in a chair beside the bed with her hands folded in her lap. She was wearing the same pretty dress she had worn to church, he noted, but without the hat and gloves.

"Hi," she said.

"Hi. Doc says I'm going to live."

"I know. He phoned us. Danny Phelps said to tell you how sorry he was. He couldn't tell you himself, because his furlough was up, and he had to report back."

He looked at her in surprise. "It was him shot me?"

The question made her look surprised. Then she realized he couldn't have known, since he had been unconscious. She explained what had happened.

When she finished, he said with a wry smile, "Guess he didn't do it on purpose. You can write him there's no hard feelings, but he ought to take some target practice."

They smiled at each other, and she bent forward to give him another kiss. When she straightened, he asked, "How's your mother and father?"

"Fine. They're out in the hall, waiting to see if you're well enough to have that many visitors."

His expression became guarded. "You told them?"

She nodded. "You made me promise to. They understand, Hedge. They don't like you any less." After a pause, she added reflectively, "I think Dad even likes you more, for some reason I don't understand. Like he's relieved you're not really a Marine."

"How about Barney?" he asked.

"He was upset, but he got over it when Dad explained everything. He still thinks you're the greatest guy ever."

"He here?"

She shook her head. "They don't allow kids under sixteen to visit patients."

"Oh." There was a long pause before he asked hesitantly, "How about Mr. Elmore?"

"He's waiting downstairs until we leave. They only allow three visitors at a time."

"What did he say?" Marion asked.

"Nothing. He doesn't often, you know. I really don't know how he feels, Hedge."

Marion sighed. "That's another lie I told. Nobody ever called me Hedge. I was always Marion."

After considering this, she said with a smile, "You're Hedge around here, and I don't know how you could change that now. You want to see my folks?"

"Of course," he said. "Bring them on in."

Chapter 28

When Rose led her parents into the room, Marion manfully tried to meet their eyes, but had to look away.

"I'm sorry," he said in a low voice.

"Errare humanum est," Mr. Hudkins said.

Marion looked puzzled. Mrs. Hudkins gave her husband a look mixing fondess with exasperation.

"To err is human," Rose translated. "I took Latin in high school under Dad."

"Well, I sure guess I erred," Marion said.

"What's done is done," Mr. Hudkins told him in a kindly tone. "You lacked a little judgment, Hedge, but Rose defended you with what struck us all as a reasonable argument. You couldn't very well hitchhike two thousand miles in your underwear."

Marion forced himself to meet the Latin teacher's eyes. "I feel worst about Barney," he said.

"Barney's all right," Mrs. Hudkins put in quickly. "He likes you as much as ever, Hedge."

Marion sighed. "You people are too much. I don't deserve it."

Mrs. Hudkins went over to lean down and kiss his forehead. "Just worry about getting better, Hedge, and forget everything else."

Flushing with embarrassment, he said, "I'll try, ma'am."

Mr. Hudkins said, "According to Dr. Manning, you probably can leave the hospital in two weeks. You'll stay with us until you're able to travel, of course."

His eyes misting, Marion said, "Thank you, sir."

"Incidentally, your parents have been informed, and

know you're going to be all right. They sent their love and understanding."

"How'd you know how to get in touch with them?" Marion asked puzzledly.

"Only one Hedgepeth with a phone in Crystal City, Missouri. Soon as Dr. Manning phoned that you were awake and in good condition, Rose got the number through information."

Looking up at Rose with love in his eyes, Marion said, "Thanks." His eyes became even more misty.

In a gentle voice Mrs. Hudkins said, "I think Hedge has had enough excitement for one night. We'd better let him get his rest."

Marion made no objection, because he was beginning to feel a little tired, and he still had another ordeal ahead of him. He said, "I'm still up to seeing Mr. Elmore for a minute. You'll send him up, won't you?"

Rose said, "Of course."

She glanced at her parents with an indecisive expression on her face, then squared her shoulders and walked over to the bed with determination. She bent to give Marion a thorough kiss on the lips.

"Night, Hedge," she said. "See you tomorrow."

The kiss had turned his face beet red, but he managed to smile at her and then to look at her parents. "Thanks for everything," he said to them.

Particularly for Rose, he was thinking, but was too timid to say it aloud.

About ten minutes after Rose and her parents left, Mr. Elmore came into the room. His face was expressionless as he walked over alongside the bed to look down at the patient. Marion forced himself to meet the railroad man's gaze, humbly prepared to accept as deserved whatever recrimination the man heaped on him.

Mr. Elmore said tonelessly, "Understand you are doing well."

"Yes, sir. Dr. Manning expects me to recover."

Dipping his right hand into the side pocket of his suit coat, Mr. Elmore produced the gold watch and chain. He set them on the bedside stand.

"Little water got in your watch," he said. "I took the liberty of having a Riverton jeweler clean the works so they wouldn't rust."

Marion looked from the watch up into the railroad man's face. "You should keep it," he said huskily. "You gave it to a Marine corporal, not to me."

The man's head moved back and forth in a slow shake. "I gave it to a young man I wanted to have it, not to a uniform."

"You're not beholden," Marion insisted uncomfortably.

"Never in my life gave a gift because I felt beholden," Mr. Elmore informed him.

Marion was impelled to smile, and got a faint, reserved smile in return.

"I said the first time you gave it to me, I'd try to deserve it, sir. I really will."

"You deserve it already," Mr. Elmore told him. "Whatever you do hereafter is a bonus." After a long pause, he asked, "What will you do when you leave here?"

"The Army, I guess. It's not the Marines, but I'd rather be that than Navy."

A faint, faraway look appeared in Mr. Elmore's eyes. "Johnny was Army. Anti-aircraft machine-gunner in the Coast Artillery Corps. Rank of corporal."

Marion finally understood why the sight of his uniform had had such impact on the railroad man. It hadn't been the Marine green, but the corporal's stripes. He understood even more when Mr. Elmore added reflectively, "About your size, too."

Not knowing what to say to this, Marion said nothing. The near show of emotion seemed to embarrass Mr. Elmore, because he cleared his throat and abruptly changed the subject.

"The doctor said not to let you get overtired, Hedge. May I come again?"

"Anytime you wish, sir. I'll be honored to have you."

Mr. Elmore gave him a formal nod. "Good night, Hedge. I wish you a speedy recovery."

"Thank you, sir."

After he left, Marion picked up the watch, pried open

the back and studied the mechanism which allowed adjustment for change in climate.

The Greyhound bus had been climbing steadily for some time. When the road eventually leveled out onto a plateau, the vista was much harsher than in the valley they had just left. Marion gazed out across the acres of stumps, interspersed by only a few scrubby trees.

It had not changed any in two years, he thought.

There was one change as they neared the other end of the plateau, though, and it was one he welcomed. Barbwire still surrounded the ex-logging camp and the tin-roofed huts were still there, but the camp stood empty and deserted.

As the bus went over the crest and started down the steep hill, he peered ahead at the village in the valley below. It was just turning dusk, but there was still light enough to see the two church spires, standing like sentries at either end of town, and the graveled streets lined with rows of white frame houses.

As the bus started through the business section, the marquee lights went on at the Granada Theater. The feature was *Hold that Blonde,* starring Eddie Bracken.

The lights of the Oasis Café also went on as the bus hissed to a stop at the entrance to its parking lot. Marion was the only passenger to alight. Bidwell was not even a regular bus stop, the driver had informed him when he changed busses at Salt Lake City. They would stop to let off passengers, but Riverton was the closest stop where you could get on.

The driver got off too, in order to unlock an outside luggage compartment in the side of the bus and pull out Marion's barracks bag. Setting it on the gravel, he said, "Good luck, Corporal."

"Thanks," Marion said. "Good luck to you, too."

As the driver climbed aboard again, the front door of the Oasis Café was pushed open from inside and Mr. Elmore peered out. Almost instantly he disappeared inside again, letting the screendoor slam. Marion swung the barracks bag up over his left shoulder and started across the lot toward the café.

Again the screen door opened, and this time a whole procession emerged. First Rose came out, running. She was followed more slowly by Mr. Elmore, Sheriff Wenzel and Charlie the cook. They all halted near the door to await Marion's approach, Rose a little forward of the rest.

The café's outdoor floodlight illuminated the parking lot brightly enough for all of them to be able to see the approaching Army corporal clearly. Sheriff Wenzel, standing between Mr. Elmore and the cook, peered to make out Marion's ribbons.

When the corporal got close enough to make out his ribbons, the sheriff said to the railroad man, "Infantry badge, E.T.O., Good Conduct, Bronze Star Medal. Did he write about the Bronze Star, Virgil?"

Mr. Elmore merely shook his head.

Charlie said, "G.I. haircut. Still pretty short, but better than a shaved head."

Suddenly tired of waiting, Rose ran toward Marion. Dropping his barracks bag, he held out both hands, apparently with the intention of gripping both of hers. Instead she went right between them to throw her arms about his neck.

Marion's arms went about her waist, and then they were kissing, right out in the open in front of everybody. Charlie lightly punched the sheriff on the shoulder, then took off his chef's cap and slammed it to the ground.

Rose drew back from the embrace after a time and took Marion's right hand. Marion swung the barracks bag up over his left shoulder again. As they neared the waiting men, Marion dropped Rose's hand in order to pull out his gold watch and look at it. Before putting it away again, he grinned at Mr. Elmore.

A slow smile formed on the railroad man's face.